ORIA'S GAMBIT

SORCEROUS MOONS – BOOK 2

BY

JEFFE KENNEDY

A PLAY FOR POWER

Princess Oria has one chance to keep her word and stop her brother's reign of terror: She must become queen. All she has to do is marry first. And marry Lonen, the barbarian king who defeated her city bare weeks ago, who can never join her in a marriage of minds, who can never even touch her—no matter how badly she wants him to.

A FRAGILE BOND

To rule is to suffer, but Lonen never thought his marriage would become a torment. Still, he's a resourceful man. He can play the brute conqueror for Oria's faceless officials and bide his time with his wife. And as he coaxes secrets from Oria, he may yet change their fate…

AN IMPOSSIBLE DEMAND

With deception layering on deception, Lonen and Oria must claim the throne and brazen out the doubters. Failure means death—for them and their people.

But success might mean an alliance powerful beyond imagining…

DEDICATION

To the wonderful members of SFWA, who helped me figure out the moons. All subsequent license and errors are my fault entirely.

<u>Credit</u>
Content Editor: Deborah Nemeth
Line and Copy Editor: Rebecca Cremonese
Back Cover Copy: Erin Nelson Parekh
Cover Design: Arel B. Grant, BZN Studio Designs

~ 1 ~

T HE GOLEM'S GLASSY claws flashed, arcing through the rosy light of the moon, and sliced open his throat. Blood poured down his naked body, steaming in the chill desert air. Out it flowed, sweeping around him like the bore tides of Bára. So much of it pooled around him that he began to drown in it. He strained to lift his battle axe, to cut the golem down with cold iron, but found a flower in his hands instead.

A white lily, luminescent and fragile, somehow escaping the blood that drained his life away.

The golem struck again and he shouted at it, no sound escaping. Because he had no throat left. Because he was dead.

How could he still be standing?

The golem's claws dripped crimson and its black maw yawned, glistening with glasslike fangs. It wouldn't ever die, forever coming after the Destrye until every last one of his people were dead, unless he managed to cut it down. Out of its mouth, sickly green fire blew, a lethal wind of flame that burned the crops and aqueducts. Not a golem then, but one of the Trom. Skin over bones, a humanoid spider, it grinned, lips red as the claws, hand reaching to turn him into skin without bones, nothing but pulped flesh. No, they were fingernails, enameled and jeweled. Natly's elegant hands slicing across his throat again, lips curving in a lascivious smile. With that third swipe, his head tumbled to the ground, and as she reached for his cock with those scarlet daggers of her nails, he finally managed to shout his anguish and fury.

"Your Highness?"

Lonen jerked in the hot water, the nightmare shredding around him with the spray of droplets. The servant boy gave him a wide-eyed look. Bero. The Báran lad had attended him his last time at baths, too. He was in Bára, again, cleaning up after the journey. No Trom or golems here.

Except in his tortured brain.

"Did you need something, Your Highness? You called out, but I didn't understand the words." Bero carried a stack of the much lighter colorful clothes that men of Bára wore. *Silk*, Oria had called the fabric, another thing apparently made by insects. Despite its disturbing origins, and like the addictive and tangy sweet honey she'd also introduced him to, the cloth had an exotic loveliness, more refined than anything produced in his homeland.

Like the sorceress herself, both unsettling and compelling.

"No, I'm fine." He cupped his hands and splashed water on his face. Sloppy of him, to have fallen asleep in the city of his enemy—and then failing to awaken at Bero's footfalls as he approached. Too comfortable in the soothing waters. Too many months of short sleep. Ion would have slapped him upside the head hard enough to have his brain ringing for the carelessness. But his brother was dead and gone these many weeks, reduced to boneless pulp at the simple touch of the Trom's evil hand.

"Would you care for wine or food now, King Lonen?" Bero asked in the trade tongue, setting out the soaps and oils. "Princess Oria said you're to have anything you ask for."

Luxurious baths, booze, and fine food—an excellent strategy to lull him into meekly doing the sorceress's bidding. The nightmare had served as a timely reminder of his purpose here—to save his people from destruction, not to indulge in Oria's gifts or seductive presence. He might have agreed to her startling proposal of marriage, but he'd proceed on his terms, not hers. For the sake of the Destrye and his sanity both.

"What are the chances of a decent steak?" He meant it as a joke, though the boy wouldn't know that. The Bárans didn't eat meat as a rule and, though the Destrye did, the grave losses to their livestock and wild game meant Lonen hadn't had anything worth calling a steak since before Battles of Bára.

"Princess Oria said to tell you she sent some of the hunters to find meat for you, Your Highness. It might take a few hours, however. Until then the best she can offer is some meat kept to feed the animals, and our usual fare."

Him and livestock—both pets of the Bárans. But his stomach growled, cramping with hollow pain, so he told Bero to bring whatever, enjoying the quiet when the boy went to fetch it. It seemed like years, not weeks, since he'd last visited the baths. That evening he'd washed himself clean of the ashes of too many dead before negotiating the peace treaty with Oria. Short-lived as that peace had been.

Then, as now, the elegant beauty of the underground chambers both enchanted and intimidated him. Built of carved gold and rose stone like the rest of Bára, the baths were pools of still water, several of them at varying temperatures, going from shallow to deeper than a man could stand. Elaborately carved pillars and arches supported the shadowy ceiling, the subtle light of the sconces not quite enough to illuminate it or the far corners of the room.

For a man who'd learned to jump at shadows, he found it surprisingly lulling. As evidenced by his falling asleep deeply enough to dream, though the nightmares were nothing new. The cursed things plagued him most nights. Odd to see Natly in this one, though, rather than Oria stalking him. A facet perhaps of his dramatically changed reality—exchanging one fiancée for the other. It appeared that by agreeing to marry Oria, he'd now have Natly haunting his sleep.

At least no one else had heard him cry out. He had the place to himself on this occasion. Probably the Bárans didn't bathe in the middle of the day. The baths simply remained filled, awaiting their convenience.

A shocking waste of water.

Bero returned, setting down a platter of food and a jug of wine, along with a tray of shining instruments. "Would you like me to shave you before you eat, or after, Your Highness?"

Reflexively, Lonen clapped a hand over his beard. He had no doubt he looked scruffy from his travels, and in comparison to the Báran men who were all clean shaven that he'd seen, but...

"Is that another of Princess Oria's edicts?" He asked, not bothering to disguise the sarcasm.

Bero ducked his head, clearly chagrined. "I apologize, Your Highness. Please forgive me. I did not mean to offend. When I serve the prince and folcwitas at their baths, they—"

Lonen held up a hand to stop the increasingly penitential torrent of explanation from the already nervous boy. "No apologies. I am short-tempered." He rinsed himself one last time, then rose from the water.

"Your Highness, I did not mean to abbreviate your bath." Bero sounded even more contrite.

"You didn't. I'm clean and I don't need to lie about, indulging myself." Especially not while his people could be dying by the Trom's dragon-breath while he luxuriated in deep water and napped. Oria had said she'd stop the incursions, but she'd also promised him that very thing before this. He had no reason to trust her—and plenty of evidence otherwise. Better to be ready to fight whatever battle presented itself next.

He dried himself with the cloth Bero handed him. Not the silk of the Báran garments, but likely the same source, woven thicker to be more absorbent. Nothing like the rough cotton towels the Destrye used. Then, draping the cloth around his hips, he sat on the bench next to the platter of food, pouring wine into the delicate goblet—made of *glass*, Oria had called it, supposedly formed of the endless sands that surrounded Bára—and drank deeply. Not Oria's sweet juice this time, but a potent dark blend made from fruits of the vine. The sorceress might not be watering her formerly lush rooftop garden any longer, but whatever the reasons for her choice, the rest of Bára didn't seem to be enduring similar privations. Of course, the fruits fermented for this wine were likely grown years ago. Possibly even before Bára turned her greedy gaze on Dru's once plentiful lakes.

"Go ahead and trim my hair and beard, but no shaving," he told Bero. "That's an offense against Arill."

Bero moved behind him, setting to trimming the curls that tended to spiral wildly when untamed. "Leave it long enough to tie back," he belatedly thought to tell the boy before he scooped up a chunk of cheese, dipping it in a dish of honey before taking a bite. It drove him crazy when his hair was too short to pull back, falling into his eyes all the time. Arill knew he didn't need to go any more insane than he already had.

Probably he'd started coming unhinged during the privations of the Golem wars. Plenty of Destrye warriors had. Fighting a relentless, inhuman enemy that kept coming at you, no matter how many you'd chopped into pieces, gave even the most stalwart man nightmares. Their camps at night had often rung with the shouts of men still fighting in their sleep, causing the lookouts no end of trouble sorting real alarms from phantasms.

Not every man showed the erosion of sanity immediately. Lonen hadn't suffered from the plaguing dreams until much later. Not until after he'd lost his father, two brothers, and countless men in the Battles of Bára. Not to mention the last bloodstained fragments of his idealism.

A wonder, really, that he'd held onto it that long.

No, for him the nightmares began after he met Oria, with her fragile beauty, demonic lizardling pet, and the ability to read his thoughts more easily than Lonen could decipher his brother's plans for aqueducts to save the Destrye from starvation.

Very likely she could do far more than that with her mysterious magic. She might be able to cloud or even direct his mind. That would explain how, though he'd come to Bára to exact revenge and restitution for her crimes against Dru, he'd somehow ended up agreeing to marry the witch.

As uneasy as it made him, he'd prefer to blame his decision on her magic, rather than contemplate how much of it might spring from his strange obsession with her.

Even the exotic taste of cheese and honey on his tongue evoked her vividly. The Destrye said that all roads led to Arill's temple—which, in fact they eventually did. Apparently all of his craziness led straight back to Oria. Back home in Dru, the land of his birth that he'd nearly killed himself to return to, he'd craved that flavor with much the same unreasonable longing he'd somehow attached to the woman who'd introduced him to it.

Both of which he'd been certain never to encounter again.

Wonders never ceased.

Bero trimmed his beard, then lathered and shaved his neck, throat and surrounding skin. He stepped back, watching anxiously as Lonen rubbed a hand over it. The Báran oils made the hair soft, and Bero's careful work created crisp demarcations between the hair and his skin. He probably wouldn't recognize himself reflected in still water.

"Does it meet with your approval, Your Highness?" Bero asked.

"Feels great." He nearly told the boy he didn't have to use the honorific every time—though he'd nearly gotten to the point of not looking for his late father when people used it—but he probably needed every measure of pomp he could muster among these status-conscious people. "Would you—"

He broke off at the echo of booted footsteps, and sprang to his feet, iron-headed battle axe leaping to hand. The Báran city guard who approached gave him a strange look—no doubt bemused by a nearly naked Destrye wielding the heavy, unrefined weapon in the sumptuous perfumed baths—but quickly bowed. "King Lonen, the Princess Oria would like to enter and speak with you once you've finished bathing and have dressed."

Oh sure. Exactly what he'd expected. And why in Arill not receive his erstwhile enemy and future wife in the bathing chambers of Bára?

"Tell her I'm at her disposal." At her beck and call, even, which stung his pride more than he liked. After all, he was doing this for his people, as a good king should. If he didn't find building aqueducts and shoveling manure beneath him, marrying a foreign witch shouldn't be.

The man hesitated fractionally—perhaps Lonen had snarled too much—then bowed again and stepped out.

"Your Highness, fresh clothes for you are—"

"I saw them. In a minute." He sat again, handing Bero the leather tie for his hair. His favorite one, in fact, exactly the right length and suppleness. He'd been sorry to realize he'd lost it in Bára, then bemused when Oria handed it back to him. Odd that she'd saved it all that time. The tie might be his preferred one, out of long habit, but it didn't look like much. Not like the fancy gold cords she wore in her braids. "A bit more oil in my hair, if you will, Bero, then tie it back."

He wasn't putting off dressing only to poke at Oria—or only to test how much she saw through that solid gold metal mask without eyeholes. No, he told himself, he acted out of practicality. There was simply no sense getting oil on the silk shirt, borrowed or not. If the side benefits alleviated his stinging pride, so be it.

He watched for her through the gloom, catching the exact moment she faltered at the sight of him. She didn't hesitate long, forging gamely forward, but it gave him a welcome bit of satisfaction that she saw him and that he could give her unease. Anything that awarded him an edge with the canny sorceress would be a welcome weapon.

She strode towards him in that impetuous way of hers, as if she brimmed with more energy than she could contain, crimson robes swirling about her long legs. The dragonlet, her constant companion, rode her shoulder, scales shining even whiter in contrast to the vividly colored silk, long tail wound around her arm like a series of decorative bracelets finishing at her wrist. Its green eyes shone in the dimness, as if lit from within.

Oria stopped her usual decorous and obvious distance from him, which perversely made him want to close the space between them. But he didn't, forcing himself to stay put. He'd never pressed unwelcome advances on a woman in his life, always careful of his size and strength. With Oria a slender sapling compared to the more robust Destrye women, he'd been particularly observant of her physical fragility and aware of crowding her.

Not that she credited him with any of that restraint. She wavered, well out of reach and poised to flee, as if he might seize her and tumble her to the floor. The idea had its merits—and were he another kind of man he might act on them—if only to reassure himself that she was still the same person inside. Innumerable sorceresses hid behind those featureless gold masks and the crimson robes of their office, virtually identical from any distance. He recognized Oria by her scent of night-blooming lilies, her low musical voice, and that bright copper hair that shone in the elaborately coiled braids. Also no one else carted about a winged, white dragonlet. But none of that substituted for seeing her.

When he'd met her before, she hadn't been a priestess and wore no mask. He missed Oria's lovely oval face and, most of all, her expressive eyes, so full of life and nearly the same color as her metallic hair. Maybe he'd carried anger for too many things for far too long, but all too familiar rage coiled in his gut that she'd glibly offered him marriage then coolly informed him that their alliance would be in name only, that he'd never share her bed or body.

Not only would he give up a normal marriage to a woman of his own people, he'd also never satisfy that unreasonable and burning desire to strip Oria naked and feel her slim body beneath his, to touch that fair skin, watch her extraordinary copper eyes darken with pleasure. Surely Arill had devised this torture in punishment for the many profane deeds he'd committed in the name of war, to bind him in marriage with the one woman who'd obsessed him like no other, and simultaneously ensure he'd never taste the single reward that might make tying himself to his foreign enemy bearable.

When Oria didn't speak, instead remaining rigidly silent and caressing her pet's tail where it looped around her wrist—a nervous gesture, to be sure—it occurred to him that she'd likely glimpsed that potent fantasy in his mind, along with his fury. Overheard how part of him howled to strip her of those shapeless robes and find the luminous slip of a candlelit woman who'd caught his eye in a window and reminded him of the fantastic tales of his boyhood, even amidst the blood, gore, and terror. Too late for her to unsee it, in that case. Teach her to snoop in his brain.

"You wanted to speak to me?" He prompted.

"I thought you were finished bathing." She shifted on her feet, masked face turned away, voice stilted. "I apologize for catching you undressed."

"I am finished," he told her, enjoying her unease far more than he should—though it rankled that she couldn't even bear to look at him. He was scarred yes, but he'd earned those fairly battling *her* golems, and if he'd grown overly skinny, that too was her fault. "Does it matter how I'm dressed—can you even see through that thing?"

"Bero, leave us, please," she said, instead of answering.

The boy patted the spiral tail of Lonen's hair and bowed his way out. Lonen poured more wine and held out the glass to her. "Wine? I've only the one glass and I drank from it, but you could sip from the other side, if you're concerned about catching a disease from me."

~ 2 ~

"NO, BUT THANK you for the offer," Oria managed to reply with reasonable politeness, proud of her even tone in the face of all the violent emotion whirling off him like sand thrown by a dust devil.

The Destrye king shrugged his bare shoulders, took a swig of the wine and popped some honey-dipped cheese into his mouth, chewing vigorously. His granite eyes stayed hard, studying her, his dislike of her mixing with sexual desire that carried an unsettling edge of fury.

As much as she'd come to appreciate the rational, even noble aspects to his character, it wouldn't pay to forget that Lonen, though king now, was a warrior first, and from a brutal, barbarian people. And his sexual nature affected her in improbable ways. Seeing with sgath wasn't the same as looking with her eyes. In some ways, it showed more details to her mind's eye—the physical lines of the man, yes, also layered with his shimmering personal vitality.

"You could take the mask off, if that's what's stopping you," he said. "It's good wine. So is the food, if you want some."

"Thank you, I've eaten." She sounded stiff, even to herself. Better that, though, than an emotional meltdown. "And my mask is a badge of office. I don't remove it, except with close family." Something she'd told him already.

"We're going to be family." Lonen swirled another hunk of cheese in the honey liberally, a gesture somehow suggestive, then ate it. His strong throat, skin newly shaved below his neat beard, moved as he swallowed, drawing her attention. Though she fought that fascination, better to look there than at the rest of him, so liberally displayed to her mind's eye.

He sat with his knees wide, the white drying cloth parting over one thigh, revealing shadows beneath. Strangely she longed to touch him, though she knew doing so would only overload her senses, causing devastating mental and even physical pain that could send her into a faint at best. He enticed her anyway, inciting a craving to caress that tanned skin, feel the dark hair sprinkled over his arms and legs, denser on his chest, then arrowing towards the cloth that could be so easily tugged away.

She blushed at the uncharacteristically prurient impulse, glad of the mask that hid it, though Chuffta would know her thoughts.

"And wouldn't judge you for them," her Familiar said in her mind. *"It's good to want your mate. It's the natural order of things."*

There would be nothing natural about this marriage. "We won't be family like that," she said aloud, to both of them. "We discussed that already and you agreed to a marriage in name only, King Lonen. I have good reasons for it."

Irritation flickered out of him, but he glanced down at the food tray, thick dark lashes hiding his eyes as he picked through the offerings, at last choosing spray of grapes. "But you haven't explained them. Nor did you answer my question about how well you can see in that mask. Even if we won't share a bed, we will share hopefully long lives bound together. We shouldn't have secrets between us."

She laced her fingers together, holding herself more rigid than she needed to. Oh, he had no idea of the secrets she kept. Chief and most dangerous among them that she could use male magic, the more active grien, along with sgath. Of course Lonen wouldn't know the difference as any of her people would, but he might slip up and say the wrong thing. Or use the information to deliberately betray her, if it became useful for him to do so.

Execution could be a handy way to dispose of an unwanted wife. If her own people did the deed for him, so much more convenient.

Since she'd gained her mask, she'd gotten much better at handling the emotional energy that she absorbed from other people as passively as she did from all living things and the deep source of magic below Bára. But dealing with it effectively meant venting the accumulated energy as grien—something she needed not only privacy, but quiet and concentration to accomplish. All of which did not come easily around the larger-than-life Destrye with his exuberant masculinity.

"Let me help." Chuffta leaned his angled cheek against the patch of skin behind her ear bared by her upswept hair, where the mask did not cover. The derkesthai's buffering abilities took the jangling energy down several notches.

"Thank you." This time she kept her reply to her Familiar private. The way Lonen's flinty eyes went to Chuffta, however, showed he suspected they conversed. Something he didn't at all like. She might be more efficient to catalog what he *did* like and consign the rest to beyond her control.

"We *will* have secrets between us," she corrected the Destrye. "For many reasons. Not all the secrets are mine alone, and the temple guards hers closely. Only those who have taken the mask may know them. Not only by sacred law, but because of a … a need for maturity in ability to absorb the information."

A wry, humorless grin cracked his face, teeth white in the dim, golden light and the darkness of his beard. "Did you just say that I'm too stupid to understand the answers to my questions?"

It sounded bad, put that way. Oria herself had only recently proved herself a master of *hwil*, a state of such perfect, inviolable peacefulness of mind and spirit that she could be trusted with the dangerous secrets of manipulating magic. Never mind that she'd lied to the priestesses and faked *hwil* well enough to pass their tests. Something else impossible to explain to an outsider, much less this brusque warrior.

Lonen could never hope to penetrate the temple's secrets. In fact, he'd be far safer and likely happier not knowing the dark side of Báran magic.

She couldn't tell him as much, however. They might be virtual strangers, but it didn't take long familiarity with the man to know he wouldn't take any explanation along those lines at all well.

She deliberately laced her fingers together again, mimicking a serenity she'd never feel, choosing her words carefully. "Even though you'll be my husband, you will still be Destrye and I will be Báran. There are worlds of things we'll never know or understand about each other. We must resign ourselves to that reality now."

His intention sharpened, giving her warning, but he still surprised a gasp out of her when he lunged to his feet and closed the distance between them with only a few athletic strides. Chuffta spread his wings and hissed, though he didn't breathe fire. Oria held her ground—barely—and Lonen flicked a dismissive gaze at her Familiar.

"Rest easy, dragonlet," he murmured. "I won't harm your mistress."

"I told you before—his name is Chuffta."

Lonen didn't acknowledge that, sticking up three fingers, his thumb and pinky tucked into his palm. "How many fingers am I holding up?"

"Lonen—"

"You're not telling me any of your precious temple secrets." He seethed with a dark combination of frustration and desire. Probably he wouldn't harm her. Not intentionally, but his longing to touch her was as palpable as the scent of warmed oils on his damp hair and skin—and as vivid as those sexual images that burned through his mind like meteors. An outsider like him might never understand what harm he could do her with the intensity of his thoughts alone, intentionally or not.

"How many fingers, Oria?" he grated out the question, his angry impatience even harsher than the sound. "It's a simple question. One I'd ask any of my men who got knocked upside the head."

It wasn't simple. None of this was.

"Three," she answered, knowing that only satisfied one question among many, but nevertheless hoping he'd let at least this go.

He nodded, confirming something to himself. Then circled around her, holding up his hand behind her. No such luck that he'd drop the subject so easily. "How many now?"

Ignorant of Báran magic, perhaps, but a canny man. Another priestess might lie, might keep the temple secrets from a foreigner, but she couldn't bring herself to deceive him more than she already had. He did deserve to know something of who—and what—he'd agreed to bind himself to.

"One."

"Is the dragonlet telling you that? It's looking at me. You can talk to it, can't you?"

"*Chuffta?*" She emphasized her Familiar's name.

Lonen made an aggravated sound. "Fine. Chuffta."

"He's protective. He doesn't like you behind my back. And yes, we communicate. Go over to the bench, Chuffta," she said aloud, for Lonen's benefit. "And look the other direction."

Chuffta grumbled without words, but did as she bid, settling on the bench, folding his wings, and delicately sniffing at the haft of Lonen's axe propped there. Her Familiar understood that she needed to build trust with her future husband—had, in fact, been lecturing her on the topic.

"*Advising you,*" Chuffta corrected. "*Which, I might point out, is my job.*"

"*Yes, yes—now let me do mine.*"

She had to force herself to hold still as Lonen drew up close behind her, the fine hairs prickling on the back of her neck. "You're holding up two fingers, one on each hand."

The man moved soundlessly, but even without sgath revealing the energies around her, his masculine aura would impact her from even much farther away. This close, it enveloped her as surely as a physical embrace, the complicated interplay of his thoughts and emotions strumming over her nerves. As disastrous as that would be, she found she ached for his touch on her skin, her body heating and throbbing as if he already had. He'd brought that out in her from the beginning, though it made no sense. Only her ideal mate—a priest, masked and trained in grien—could interact with her the right way, without harming her.

She'd only completed the first stages of testing—meshing auras to evaluate compatibility. None of the priest candidates had affected her like this. Though that could be because none had met the initial requirements either. Perhaps an ideal husband would affect her this way?

Not that it mattered. These feelings for a foreigner were … unnatural. A perversion born of her adolescent fascination with the gruesome illustrations of the barbaric Destrye warriors carrying off naked women to do vague and illicit things to them. She could never explain why those stories mesmerized her—before the priestesses snatched them away as inappropriate—no more than she could prevent her body from rousing to Lonen's presence and the potent sexuality that surrounded him.

However, though she might not have true *hwil*, she created the appearance of it well enough to fool the High Priestess. She could and would just as easily fool this magicless Destrye and prevent him from ever knowing how he affected her.

Allowing any glimpse of her weakness would only encourage him to pursue the topic of bedding her, and that could never happen. He'd touched her once—on the wrist—and she'd been unconscious for a week. She couldn't imagine what sexual intimacy would do to her. No matter how much this newly discovered, recklessly sexual side of her wanted it.

"What do you want, Oria?" Lonen breathed the question close to her ear, startling her into thinking for a moment that he'd turned the tables and read *her* mind. "Why did you come here?" he clarified. "I thought it was difficult for you to leave your tower."

Grateful to be back to non-sexual and non-magical business, she seized the opportunity to step away and turn to face him. She didn't need to, of course, but it helped diffuse that heady intimacy, the implicit trust of having him behind her, his body heat warm on her back, his breath on her exposed nape.

"I can leave my tower more often than when you knew me before. I am … stronger now."

"Because of the mask."

"It's more that I have the mask because I'm stronger."

He contemplated that, studying her. "Is the hair part of it?"

She stumbled mentally. "The hair?"

Lonen waved his hands, indicating her elaborate hairstyle by wiggling his fingers, transmitting a fair amount of Destrye disdain for all things Báran. "The braids and stuff."

She put a hand to the intricately woven style, though she hardly needed to confirm its existence to herself. "It's just easier, with the mask ribbons, to tie it all together. Well, and it's traditional."

"I liked your hair better when you wore it down."

Dropping her hand, she straightened. "I'm not a decoration that exists to please you, King Lonen."

"Not in bed, nor out of it," he replied, both musing and taunting.

"Enough of that." She was losing patience for this … sparring match. That's what it was. "It's not too late to back out of the deal. Don't marry me. I understand if this one caveat is too much to ask." She sneered a little though, when she said it. He could have all the women he wanted. She'd be the one committing herself to a life of never knowing the touch of another person besides her mother.

"And me."

"A human person," she amended with a mental caress of affection. Again she was glad of the mask that hid her smile. Lonen had folded his arms, glaring at her. He would only grow more annoyed if he thought she laughed at him or took their predicament lightly.

"Hardly one simple caveat. However, as you so succinctly

pointed out," he was saying, biting out the words, "I don't have a choice in this. You can't save the Destrye from the Trom unless you're married to the Destrye king, because that's how the magic works." He freed a hand to wave it in the air, much as he had in describing the braids, making the magical rules seem equally fussy.

That's what she'd told him, a convenient half-lie. In truth, getting him to marry her had a great deal more to do with becoming Queen of Bára, granting her access to the innermost secrets that would enable her to summon the Trom and wrest control of them from Yar. Guilt chewed at her, though. She'd been thinking on her feet. How much of her conniving Lonen into marriage came from her strange attraction to him?

It worried her that she'd made the decision, not out of integrity and the resolution to live up to her promises, but out of self-indulgence. A family trait and failing, perhaps. One that had led Bára into taking so much at the cost of others.

She should face this potential corruption of her moral fiber. She did feel that, when Lonen wasn't pissed at her, they shared some common ground, besides this impossible attraction. Though they'd admittedly conversed very little—and she'd spent an awful lot of her life alone so she had little to compare—she liked talking with him better than anyone else she'd met.

"Besides me."

"A human person!" But she laughed in her head, no doubt as Chuffta intended.

"You're laughing at me." Lonen flung the accusation at her, granite eyes flat.

"No!" She retorted, too fast, surprised into being defensive. He knew it, too, narrowing his eyes at her. Worse and worse. She scrambled to explain. He wouldn't much like the truth, but he'd flustered her too much to think up a good excuse on the spot. "Chuffta and I do more than communicate—he talks to me. And sometimes he's … he makes jokes. In my head."

Chuffta flipped his wings at Lonen's incredulous stare. "You're saying the dragonlet is a smartass?"

She couldn't help it—maybe it was all the tension—but she laughed in truth. Lonen transferred his bemused stare to her, anger lightening. "I've never heard you laugh before."

"Surely you have."

"Not a real laugh, like that one, instead of those little huffing noises you make when you find something ridiculous." A mischievous smile tugged at his mouth, one she recalled from when he'd teased her about using that sword she could barely lift.

"I do not make huffing noises," she protested, and he pointed a finger.

"There. Exactly like that one."

"How did you even know I was laughing at what Chuffta said? I didn't make any sound, huffing or otherwise."

He cocked his head slightly, his smile fading and his face growing serious again. "You may be wearing a mask and that ugly shapeless robe, but I can still see the lines of your body, how you move and hold yourself."

Oh. She didn't know what to do with that information. His own way of sensing emotion, she supposed. A warrior's way of reading an opponent. He stood there, relaxed hands on towel-draped hips, and watched her, waiting for her to speak next.

She should tell him the truth, that she could marry his brother and it should work magically. That she'd misled him because she herself would rather marry a man she knew and felt affinity for. Her feelings weren't important. She was forsworn and must make recompense. It didn't matter that it had been Yar who had broken her promise that the Trom, the ancient guardians of Bára, would leave the Destrye in peace. Only a recreant would try to dodge the guilt by claiming it wasn't her fault. It fell to her to make good on the promise, not to find a path through her penance that pleased herself.

Time, however, *was* of the essence. If Yar returned from one of their sister cities with an ideal mate, he'd make a temple-blessed marriage and his claim to the crown would trump hers. If she could get Lonen to marry her that very evening, she might beat Yar to the crown. Under false pretenses. But for the right reasons. It was all a mire deeper than the muddy Bay of Bára when the tides receded.

To give herself time to mull the ramifications, she moved over to Chuffta, stroking his arched neck.

"Here—come meet Chuffta officially. He's a derkesthai and does not much like you calling him a dragonlet or a lizardling. You can touch him."

"Did I say I wanted to?"

"You said you wanted to know more about me. Here's something to know."

Trepidation colored Lonen's energy, until he shook it off. He drew near, then extended a fingertip and traced the luminously white scales. The anger evaporated entirely for the moment, leaving behind a shimmering wonder. "He's soft," he said reverently. "And intelligent?"

"Very. He has a tendency to lecture."

"My job," Chuffta reminded her unnecessarily.

"He scolds you?"

"Yes, as he's reminding me now that it's his job as my Familiar."

"I've never heard the word used that way—what does it mean?"

"It means that he's family to me, that he ... helps me." So difficult to explain to this hard man all the ways she was fragile, how Chuffta buffered the worst of the impacts of incoming energy. "It's a special relationship."

"Do you remember the first time I saw you?" Lonen asked, voice rapt as he stroked Chuffta's curved neck.

Though an apparent non-sequitur, his question made perfect sense to Oria. It had been the first time she saw him, too. "Through the window." She'd been transfixed by the sight of him, blood-drenched axe in one hand, knife in the other, as he slaughtered the priestesses on the walls, helpless in their trances as they fed sgath to the battle mages. They'd died easily because none of those women had active grien as the men did. As Oria did, against all nature and common sense—a secret no one but her mother and Chuffta could know.

Unless Yar had guessed, which could spell disaster.

"I'd never seen anything like you in my life." Lonen wasn't looking at her, his emotional energy turning warm, a youthful, wondering feel to him, his voice almost dreamy. "You and your derkesthai, like something out of an illustration in an old storybook. Fantastical and ethereal. Magical."

She stroked Chuffta's wing, holding her breath against confessing that Lonen had looked to her like something that stepped out of a book, too. Ironic that his vision had an innocent, even romantic purity to it while hers had carried darkly sexual overtones—particularly given their current opposition where she'd play the eternal virgin and he could cat about as much as he pleased.

"Why can you touch Chuffta and not me?"

His question caught her by surprise and she realized he'd transferred his gaze to her face, focus intent on her, as if he tried to see through the mask.

"It's an ... energy thing," she replied, far too breathlessly. Not a useful trick, long term, to hold her breath as a way of holding her tongue. She'd have to find something else.

"An energy thing." His hand strayed much too close to hers on Chuffta's hide.

She snatched hers away and tucked both hands behind her back. "Well, energy and magic and ... emotion."

"That goes through the skin." His voice had hardened, a step short of calling her a liar.

"I tried to explain that you wouldn't understand."

"I touched you once before, at the city gates when you surrendered to me."

Something about the way he said that made heat wash over her. "I surrendered Bára to you, not myself."

"You're one and the same, just I am myself, and also the Destrye and also Dru."

"Whatever you're driving at, even after we're married—should you decide to go forward with that plan—you will never be able to touch me without hurting me, so decide carefully."

His attention sharpened, a hint of dismay to it. "Did I hurt you before?"

Better to be candid. "Yes."

"And that's why you fainted—and were ill for a week."

Tempting to tell him yes and put a forever end to this line of inquiry, but she didn't like lying to him. Not outright. Not more than she had to. "That was part of it, but not all."

"Because I made you go outside the walls."

"Yes, that was another part. I can't leave Bára."

He stilled, outraged astonishment buffeting her. "Then how do you propose to be Queen of the Destrye?"

It hadn't occurred to her that he'd had some idea of taking

her with him to Dru. "I—I don't know," she replied, far too faintly.

"I'm to tell my people their queen will never set foot in their forests?" His voice rose in volume on the question, his incredulous frustration hammering at her.

Oria threw up her hands, giving in to the urge to pace, to release the restless feelings he stirred up, a mirror to his. A break in *hwil*, but he wouldn't have any way to know that. "Don't tell them you married me at all! I don't care. Marry your Natly and have her play your queen."

"You said it matters to the magic, that you are bound to the Destrye king."

"It does. But what occurs on the magical plane doesn't have to be exactly replicated on the human one. What matters is that you marry me in our temple, that we're bound by oath and magic. I don't care if you marry Natly, too…in whatever kind of temple you have."

He stared at her for one more long, incredulous moment, then appeared to snap. With an abrupt turn, he stalked over to the pile of clothes, tossed aside the drying cloth, and yanked on the pants with furious gestures.

Though Oria averted her gaze automatically, her sgath worked largely on a subconscious level, constantly feeding her information about her surroundings—including a far too detailed vision of how Lonen looked naked.

"Arill take you, Oria," he snarled. "You sure know how to piss me off."

How she longed for a swig of that wine.

~ **3** ~

HE'D NEVER FIGURED himself for a romantic. Even when he was merely a prince and third in line for the throne, he'd known that although he didn't have to marry for duty—the Destrye did not engage in complicated politics, as the Bárans did—any bride he chose would have been subject to his father's blessing. Sure, he and Natly had talked about marriage, but looking back, he could see that he'd felt safe coaxing her about it, indulging in the flirtation of it, knowing she'd never say yes. Her ambitions had looked higher than that. She'd sulked for weeks when his oldest brother, Ion, married Salaya.

After that she'd worked her wiles on the second-oldest, Nolan, until he firmly rebuffed her flirtations—not only because King Archimago had decidedly *not* approved of her. Only then had she returned to Lonen. He hadn't minded her fickle games. Natly was beautiful, with an arsenal of sensual tricks that turned a man's mind, and he enjoyed her playful company. But chasing her had been a good deal more fun than having her. Those weeks in Dru after he returned home from the war, reluctantly taking up the crown that should never have been his in the natural order of things, Natly had affixed herself to his side, talking of nothing but the midwinter wedding ceremony he'd never quite agreed to. He hadn't really meant to lie to Oria by calling Natly his fiancée. After all,

Natly figured them to be engaged and he'd never directly disabused her of the notion. He'd simply never found the energy to make a decision one way or the other.

He'd put it down to exhaustion—mental and physical—from tackling the Destrye's many problems. More than enough decisions to make there, few of them optimistic. That soul-deep weariness from all he'd done had made Natly's lighthearted ways, the ones he'd once prized, seem somehow tawdry and frivolous.

He'd already been battling the realization that it would be irresponsible of him as king to make Natly queen when Arnon put it into words. *You can't marry her. She would have made a decent princess, but she won't make a good queen.* Part of him had even felt relief at finding a way out. Arnon didn't outrank him, but his brother had a good brain and knew how to use it. It would take substantial conviction to ignore his one remaining brother's advice. Perhaps he also channeled their father's stern ghost.

He'd agreed to Oria's extraordinary proposal in part because he knew she *would* make a good queen, even if she was a Báran sorceress who'd bewitched him. She'd demonstrated the resolve, courage, and selflessness to sacrifice herself for any people she took as her own. It had seemed fitting to him, a restoring of balance, that she'd step in to take responsibility for the Destrye when King Archimago had died taking responsibility to protect vulnerable Bárans.

It hadn't occurred to him that she didn't intend to act as queen for anyone but the Bárans.

And now she glibly announced that she didn't care if he took another wife, if another woman pretended to be the Destrye queen in her place. That was the final snowflake to bring down the tree limb.

He pulled the shirt over his head, settling the wide collar, and found she'd stopped her pacing and regained her regal poise, handing him a full glass of wine.

"Perhaps you'll explain your anger to me," she said, all polite elegance. "A calm and rational conversation should not be too much to ask."

Taking the glass, he swallowed a healthy portion. Finding himself unable to match her reserve just yet, he stalled. "Just why *are* we standing in the baths having a long conversation, Oria?"

She gestured to the many benches. "You are welcome to sit. I came here to discuss next steps with you in private, as I had other tasks nearby, and I thought to save you the trouble of climbing to my tower again."

He grimaced at that. It had taken a good quarter-hour to ascend those endless curving stairs to her terrace atop the tallest tower in Bára. "What next steps?"

Spreading her palms wide, she huffed her exasperation. He supposed she made that sound when it wasn't a half-laugh, too. Before, when she hadn't had a metal mask hiding her face, she'd kind of puffed out her lips when she did it, blowing out her breath as if she released some tension. "The next steps are moot, Lonen, if we're not going to marry."

"Oh, we're getting married all right." His turn to pace. "We agreed already. But mark me on this: I will not be in violation of my vows by marrying or bedding anyone besides you. I can't imagine what you think of my honor as a man and a king, but I don't make promises, then turn around and break them."

"I don't either," she said quietly.

"Don't you? You promised to be Queen of the Destrye then informed me you'll never go to Dru and you're fine with a false queen on the throne, regardless of how well she'd serve the people."

Oria's golden mask seemed to ripple with flame as she swung her head to face him. He imagined her pretty mouth hanging open in an O of surprise. "I hadn't thought of it that way." To her credit, she sounded chagrined, which helped mollify him.

"Clearly." He polished off the wine, then grabbed a hunk of bread to help soak up the alcohol in his blood. The Bárans made excellent bread, he had to give them that.

"Though I did assume, when you said you were engaged, that you'd chosen a fiancée who'd make a good queen," she pointed out, with cool logic that stung a little. He couldn't explain that he hadn't given it much thought without sounding like the idiot he was, so he made a show of chewing the bread.

"I thought you'd be pleased enough to keep Natly as your lover—or wife according to your customs—and go on your way," Oria continued, in a tone of infinite patience that didn't fool him for a moment. "Some barbarian cultures allow a man to have multiple wives and concubines, I understand. A marriage of state that benefits you politically while not tying you down personally should be welcome to you."

He decided not to touch the condescending "barbarian cultures" remark. Particularly since the Destrye had maintained such practices in the past.

"For someone whose name you heard once, you've certainly mentioned Natly numerous times." He couldn't help taunting her with that. Oria might not want him to touch her, but she didn't like the idea of Natly having him either, much as she protested otherwise.

"Because she's constantly in the forefront of your thoughts," Oria retorted.

He shook his head at her, pleased to have caught her out. "Oh, Oria. Now that's a lie."

She didn't reply immediately. "That doesn't matter. I concede the point—if we decide to go ahead with this marriage and you want me to truly be Queen of the Destrye, I'll do what I can. I've learned a great deal, maybe I can eventually find a way to travel there. You're correct—I owe that much to you and Dru. But have you thought of how your people will feel about having a Báran sorceress among them, affecting their laws, passing judgment on them?"

"If you manage to drive off the Trom and put food in their mouths, they'll be happy enough." He repressed a shudder at the thought of those skeletal monsters who could at that moment be riding their fire-breathing dragons to burn the Destrye crops and buildings before they stole more of Dru's precious water. His people would put up with more than a foreign queen to be rid of that curse. "If the price is marrying their king to you so you can work your magic to protect them, then even Arill cannot deny your fitness to wear the wreath of royalty."

She sighed and held out a hand. For a moment his heart tripped in ridiculous pleasure; he thought she invited him closer. But no, the dragonl—Chuffta—flew to her. The left forearm and shoulder of her crimson robe were padded, allowing the creature to land with his back talons gripping and wide white wings spread until he balanced. She scratched his breast, her body taking that intimate posture she probably wasn't consciously aware of, which betrayed that she conversed with her Familiar. To salve his disappointment and irrational jealousy that she lavished affection on her pet and not him, Lonen savagely chewed more bread. At least he wouldn't be so blazingly hungry. Not for food, anyway.

"There's something I should tell you," she said.

"Does that mean you're relenting on withholding information? Or confessing to a previous lie?" He tensed for the answer, having placed a great deal of trust in Oria's basic honesty, if nothing else. How much more a fool would he be proved to be before this was done?

"I admit haven't told you everything. I never *will* tell you everything, which might be misleading if not an outright lie, so if that's your line in the sand, we might as well call off the agreement now."

"You're awfully insistent on not getting married now," he noted. "This was your idea to begin with."

"I know. But I was not completely forthcoming with you and I should have been." She took a deep breath and squared her shoulders. "I *could* marry your brother instead. Connecting to any part of the ruling family should be the same. That would leave you free to marry Natly"—she held up a hand when he opened his mouth—"or another. Someone who would be a *real* queen for your people. It was unfair and wrong of me not to offer that."

She cast a glance at Chuffta while Lonen mulled over her words, making him wonder what her Familiar counseled.

"Then why did you insist earlier that it had to be me?'

Oria sighed, mask turned away, though with her uncanny perceptions she'd know exactly where he was, what he was doing. How he felt. Though maybe not entirely. She didn't seem to sense how much of his willingness to marry her had nothing to do with duty at all. Something that might be best to conceal from her, lest she use it as yet another weapon against him.

"Several reasons," she said, her words followed by a heartfelt sigh. "All of them self-serving. I am not Queen of Bára because I can't be crowned until I'm married. Fortunately, neither can the only other viable contender, my brother Yar, whom you no doubt remember."

He did. Yar was younger than Oria and still a boy in most respects, with a voice that cracked and the brash impetuousness of too much arrogance and too little experience. Still, Yar had helped Lonen's warriors after the Trom attack, using his truly spectacular magical skills to mold stone into bridges and shelters. An ability like that, no matter how unsettling, would come in handy for building, say, aqueducts that didn't burn.

Oria began pacing again. Chuffta hopped to a nearby bench, watching her. "Right now, Yar is away looking for a bride from one of our sister cities. If he returns with an ideal— a suitable match, he'll be married before I can be and the throne will be his."

Lonen scratched his beard thoughtfully, its trimmed and oiled softness an unfamiliar sensation. "Not to be callous about your ambitions, but would that be such a terrible thing?"

She laughed, this one bitter with a metallic echo. "You think I'm power hungry and crave the throne. I suppose that's a fair assumption on your part."

Actually he didn't think that at all. It didn't mesh with what little he did know about her, and he felt obscurely ashamed of hurting her by the implication. He opened his mouth to say... something, but she forged on in a rush, wringing her pale fingers together.

"I did not send the Trom to Dru, but someone in Bára did. The ways of the Trom are mysterious even to us, but they can be directed by their summoner. It doesn't make sense, but I think it had to be Yar who sent them. He's the one who summoned them originally and he must control them still. He has powerful allies on our council and in the temple, those who believe it's far easier to continue to steal water from the Destrye than to cast about for other options. We also face problems with our sister cities, because we've been supplying them with water—your water—and trading goods and political favors for it. That leverage is part of how Yar will be able to convince them to give him one of their priestesses for a bride. I don't have a particular yen to be Queen of Bára, but I desperately don't want Yar to be king. For the good of the Destrye, you don't either. With the power of the throne of Bára and the sister cities *and* the Trom under his command…" she shook her head. "I don't care to picture that future. I thought you might understand."

He considered the torrent of information, as overwhelming as heavy rain on parched earth. When she decided to confide, she did so full out, something that put him in mind of her restless, energetic stride.

"So your solution is to marry ahead of him and be crowned before he returns," Lonen summarized for them both. A solid plan, but what had been her intention before he turned up at Bára's gates only hours ago? She had to have had something else in mind. "Why doesn't he marry a Báran girl—priestess, that is? Or the same for you—if time is of the essence, that would be easier and faster. You claimed you didn't have another man lined up to marry. Did you withhold information there also?" A not-so-surprising twinge of possessiveness at that thought. Though he'd never truly contemplated having Oria for himself, not beyond those plaguing dreams and the occasional fantasy, not until she proposed it.

"No—that's the full truth. I don't have anyone to marry because it's not that easy." She tucked her hands in the small of her back, pacing fast enough to make the crimson silk billow around her legs. "It's difficult to explain."

"Try," he suggested in a dry tone, and her mask flashed as she glanced at him.

"I don't think you're stupid or ignorant. But I *do* know you're skeptical about certain elements of magic and how it works."

"Acknowledged." He poured the rest of the honey over another hunk of bread, scraped the dregs with a piece of cheese and piled several more on. A slice of meat and it would be a decent sandwich. As it was, he might never stop eating.

"The temple matches us with our spouses. In the best of all possible worlds, we find a ... good fit and make a temple-blessed marriage."

"An arranged marriage."

"More than that—there's complex testing that involves magic." She waved that off as yet another thing he wouldn't understand. Probably he wouldn't, but it rankled nonetheless. "Sufficeto say Yar did not find a match in Bára. With so many of our priestesses lost in the battle with, well, with your people..." She took a breath, and he understood the feeling. The memories of that night pained him, too. He'd been the one to kill most of those priestesses, and their blood still soaked his nightmares. Oria had seen him with that blood on his hands. No wonder she didn't want them and those stains of murder on her unsullied skin.

"There are far fewer candidate priestesses in Bára now, and none satisfied the requirements for Yar, so he's casting his net wider," Oria said more briskly. "I've received my mask recently, so I've only just begun testing, but I face the same scarcity with so many of our priests fallen in battle. So far the results are not promising, which surprises nobody at all even with a reduced pool, because I'm ..."

"A princess?" He filled in, when she didn't—but she shook

her head.

"Unusually sensitive, let's say." A wealth of feeling crawled beneath her dry tone. Interesting.

"But even if Yar is counting on that," he said when she didn't continue, "on you taking longer to find a match, why risk it if the throne is at stake, something he clearly *does* have his ambitions set on? Why not settle for the second- or third-best pick?" As Oria was doing in proposing to him, it suddenly hit him. A far less savory realization. The honey wasn't enough to keep the bread from going dry in his mouth.

Oria stopped in front of him, twisting her fingers together again, and he viciously wished he could see her face, read her expression. Although he supposed he didn't need to see her to know he wouldn't like her answer. "Just tell me, Oria. Truth is best."

Though he wasn't entirely sure of that.

"A mate who's a good fit is … ideal." She settled on the word with a frustrated lifting of her hands. "A temple-blessed marriage trumps one that isn't. Were Yar and I both to marry, whichever of us has the best suited partnership—as the temple evaluates such things—would be crowned."

"So not only do you need to be married first, you need to be married and crowned before Yar can return with a supposedly better marriage."

"Yes, exactly." She sounded relieved that he understood—and maybe that she'd gotten away with not telling him everything about why the Bárans sought these purportedly perfect matches. Knowing them, it had to do with power and status. And magic, more than likely. Something he did not and would never have.

He pondered letting it lie there. Couldn't. "Why haven't you stepped up your own search, gone to these other cities to find your match?"

"I was considering it," she admitted, "before you arrived. But in the first place it's much easier for men to go beyond the walls than it is for women, for complex reasons I can't explain, but they're the same ones that would make it difficult for me to go to Dru. That same … syndrome will also cause Yar delays in bringing a bride back to Bára from her home city, so that gives me breathing room."

"And in the second place?"

"I don't have the influence he does. Because I refuse to be part of trafficking stolen water."

She said it simply, but the bald integrity of her statement touched him in an odd way—more than any of Natly's declarations of love had. It hadn't been that long ago that Lonen had sat on Oria's rooftop terrace and scorned her for not knowing whose life's blood kept her lush garden alive.

"Thank you for that," he told her gravely, meaning it. She might be playing a game of omission and half-truths, but he could count on that about her, at least.

She shrugged that off, pacing away and seeming uncomfortable. He wanted to ask more about what an ideal mate for her would be, but likely it would only cause him pain to hear all the things he could not be to her. Words like that could never be unheard and would lie between them. After years of marriage, such small resentments festered and became mortal wounds. He'd seen enough of that between his own mother and father to want to avoid the same in his own marriage, if at all possible. His idealism at work again—to be contemplating a loveless, sexless marriage of state and still hoping for happiness between them. And yet perhaps it wasn't entirely blind optimism that made him think Oria pushed to marry him instead of Arnon.

"So you call your reasons self-serving because you'll get to be queen, which makes little sense since you don't really want the power or the glory."

He had the impression that she grimaced. "That—and because being queen will give me access to the highest level of temple secrets. Which will let me discover how Yar summoned the Trom, so I can do likewise. That's how I'll wrest power from Yar and relieve Dru from the Trom's incursions."

"How did Yar get access to these secrets if he's not yet king?"

She ticked a finger at him. "You're good at this. I didn't think to ask that question for some time. I'm not certain, but I think High Priestess Febe broke sacred law and gave the spell to him. Or she gave it to Nat and Nat gave it to him."

"Your brother Nat was king following your father's death, so why was that breaking sacred law?"

"Because he *wasn't* king." She made a disgusted noise and waved her hands in the air. "They told the Destrye that, but Nat wasn't married either, so the rites couldn't be performed. But Febe and the head of the non-magical side of the council, Folcwita Lapo?"

"I remember him," Lonen said with grim distaste for the overblown man.

"They both heavily favored bringing in the Trom once it became clear the city had fallen to the Destrye."

"And they now support Yar's bid for the throne."

"Not coincidentally, yes."

"So, marrying me is the expedient choice, I can see that, but how likely are they to support your claim? Why wouldn't they delay a decision for Yar's return?"

"A potential pitfall to be sure, but I have some people on my side, too. My mother, formerly queen, may have been relieved of her mask and crown, but she still holds a great deal of sway on the council, in the temple, and in the hearts of the people of Bára. Also the city guard supports her and me, which helps enormously. For example, that's how you came to be personally escorted to me without anyone else knowing you're here. Something I'd like to keep from public notice as long as possible, another reason to have this conversation here, where no one can overhear. Finally, though you declined taking a role in governing Bára when we set terms for our surrender . . ."

Her voice wavered a bit on that word, just as she'd been unsettled when he'd said it to her earlier, about having surrendered to him. She wasn't nearly as unaffected by him as she pretended to be. Perhaps he stood a chance of wearing her down on the sexless marriage concept. Surely there must be ways for their women to be touched, or there would never be babies. He might not be a Báran man, or a priest, but he knew how to pleasure a woman. If nothing else, Natly with her bold demands and sensuous nature had taught him that much.

Oria had found her composure again, her stride more measured as she paced. "The treaty might say that you did not care to exact governorship of Bára in any way, but you *are* king of the Destrye and you did conquer Bára. They won't like it, and I might have a fight on my hands, but they'll have to acknowledge that Bára, and everything and everyone in it, belongs to you, by right of the ancient laws."

A heady thought, that Oria already belonged to him. Had he been one of his rougher ancestors, he likely would have already dragged Oria back to Dru with him as a war prize, his to do with as he pleased. The lustful fantasy aroused him profoundly, appealing to some base instinct even though the more civilized part of himself stood back in horror. It made him recall fragments of those old tales though…

"There are stories," he said, pulling on the memories to bring them out, "of foreign, pale-skinned women brought home to be wives and concubines of Destrye warriors, who inexplicably faded and died. As if they starved for food none could provide. Is that what would happen to you?"

She stopped, the abrupt change in topic derailing her stride along with her thoughts, a strange cant to her body, almost as if she were in pain. Chuffta sat up higher, wings mantling as his sinuous neck moved in a sort of question. A good insight, that he reacted to Oria's thoughts and moods. Another way to puzzle her out.

"I didn't know that," she finally breathed, strain in it. "We have no such stories."

"Perhaps you wouldn't." He kept his voice soothing, nearly regretting that he'd brought it up, except that it had garnered such a telling emotional response from her. "If the women were taken away and died without returning home…"

"Yes. No one would have known what happened to them. Tell me—were they … used?"

He nearly choked at the euphemism, especially on the heels of his brutish fantasies, then wrestled with the chagrin at having to answer, to own up to what kind of people the Destrye had been before they settled in Dru, tamed by Arill's gentle hand. Maybe there was no possible way to explain. For the first time he understood what she meant, that she could give him answers, but that he wouldn't necessarily understand them. He tried to couch it gently. "If you mean, did the men who captured the women take them to bed in the marriage sense, the answer is assuredly yes."

"Of course that's what I mean," she replied in a tart tone, far better than the pained one, and amusing him that he'd tried to be delicate. "And how can you be so sure—do the stories say so?"

"Not exactly, but—" He had to clear his throat. "Why else take them?"

Her mask faced him as he answered, seeing far too much in him. "That would have contributed, too. The sex," she clarified unnecessarily, "just as it would damage me if you gave into those … impulses like you imagined just then."

Stung, he pushed to his feet. "I wouldn't," he said far too loudly, and he was further abashed when she flinched and took several steps back. He had to take a steadying breath to lower his voice. "It's not fair, Oria, that you judge me based on fleeting thoughts and emotions. People think and feel many things they don't act on. That's part of learning to be a decent human being—knowing that there are dark yearnings in your heart and being strong enough to recognize them as such and exert control. Maybe your mind is this perfect, serene place and you don't understand the human struggle to be a better person, but I'm only a man and a flawed one at that."

She swayed, seeming shocked. "I am human, Lonen."

"You don't always seem like it."

"No?" She sounded surprised and … weary. Sad and weary. "Regardless, I understand that struggle all too well. Being flawed."

"Maybe I'd know that if I could read your mind, too. But if you couldn't see so easily into my head, you would have never known I harbored any such thoughts, however temporary, to judge me so harshly for them."

She nodded, folding her hands. "I apologize for any offense. I did not mean to sit in judgment. I sense enough of you to know your better nature. If I hadn't, I wouldn't have taken this gambit. Still... this conversation has revealed much and

I'm growing more certain that it would not be a good idea for us to marry."

"Because of my sexual feelings for you?" Might as well lay it all out there.

"All right, yes. That's one reason. I'm concerned by your insistence that you would not take other lovers. I know men have … needs. It's become obvious to me that yours are quite strong." She paused, a little breathless, as if flustered. "You must understand that I'll never be able to satisfy them for you."

He took the risk of moving closer to her, fascinated that she continued with a conversation that clearly discomfited her. She lifted her chin as he approached and visibly steeled herself not to step back, so he stopped where he was. "Women have needs, too, Oria."

She tilted her head. "Do they? I'm not sure it's the same. Or perhaps it's a difference between Báran and Destrye."

He couldn't believe that. "You've never felt anything at all sexual? Nothing—never wanted to be with a man or a woman? Never have been with either?" He wasn't sure if she was playing coy, dumb, or was truly that innocent. *Or alien,* part of him cautioned.

"Same sex unions are frowned on in Bára—it puts the magic balance off. And no." Her voice sounded faint and he imagined a blush stained her high, delicate cheekbones. "A Báran priestess lies only with her husband."

"And I will be your husband," he couldn't help saying, edging closer, halting when she raised her palms.

"Not like that. If you can't agree to that part of the marriage, then we have to call it off."

"And do what?" He curled his hands into fists of frustration. "I need your help for Dru, you need to be married and made queen to do it."

"I could marry your brother," she insisted. "He would have the same freedom I offered you. I would never impose on him or interfere with his life."

"He's not here, which thwarts your need for speedy action."

"A marriage by proxy then. You could command it and the council and temple will abide. The ritual magic knows no physical distance."

He rather enjoyed debating with her, especially when she forgot to be poised and starting sounding fierce. He'd never be able to step aside and let Arnon have her. Or any man. "Same distance problem in getting him to agree, however. How could I send and receive messages in a short time? It might take considerable explanation and debate."

She flung up a hand. "I don't know. Can't you simply do it and tell him later? You're the king."

He could, yes, though Arnon would make the rest of his days a misery. "Not happening," he said, instead. "There is no way I'm standing by while you marry another man. You proposed to me and I accepted. I won't allow you to back out."

"You won't allow me." Her voice had gone lethally chill. Something swirled in the air around him that reminded him of the sorcerer's magic on the battlefield. Her slim body had gone tense as a plucked bow string and he wondered, far from the first time, what form her magic took. Shards of ice, perhaps, instead of fireballs. "How, exactly, do you plan to enforce that edict?" She asked softly, in clear warning.

He leaned in. She was scary, all right, but he found her impossibly titillating at the same time. He'd totally lost his mind, but it seemed to matter less and less. "By invoking right of ancient law. As you noted, Bára and everything in it belongs to me."

"You wouldn't dare," she hissed.

"I won't have to," he returned, "because you're far too intelligent, noble, and rational to be stubborn for the wrong reasons. I'm right here, willing and able to marry you, I'll agree to a marriage in name only, with the caveat that we'll revisit if you change your mind about that aspect in the future. The rest is details. Done."

~ **4** ~

O RIA STRUGGLED TO find a reply to that, but she'd dug herself too deep into a dune and the sands of cascading reactions showered down on her, threatening to bury her in her own conniving.

She was too new at this maneuvering—in politics and with a man. Particularly this man.

"I warned you he would not be easily led." Chuffta's mind-voice at least held a note of concern. Any smugness to his 'I told you so' might have pushed her over the edge. As it was, the male grien magic she shouldn't possess—except in a quiet ladylike seed—thrummed with the need to escape, preferably to knock the cocksure Destrye warrior off his feet. *Allow* her, indeed.

"It's not a question of changing my mind about sex," she gritted out. "That is not under my control."

Lonen held up hands in mock surrender. "All right then. Why are we even fighting about this?"

She didn't even know—she'd lost track of the entire argument. The man did things to her. Mixed her up. Made her want things she couldn't have and certainly didn't have the luxury of wanting, with so many more pressing matters. That potent sexuality of his made it difficult to think clearly. And he called her rational and intelligent. Ha! She took a step back, giving herself relief from his stimulating presence, but lifted her chin, lest he think he'd cowed her. "Probably because you're wrong; I am frequently stubborn for the wrong reasons."

A grin broke across his face, his great good humor also—thankfully—cutting that sexual tension that had swamped her. It seemed that, as he triggered the response in her, she did likewise to him. They were fools to be doing this to themselves.

"So, what was your other reason?" He asked.

"For being stubborn?"

"No." He waved that off, going back to the food platter and taking the last item on it—a bowl of greens he grimaced at but efficiently spooned into his mouth and chewed. "You said you had several self-serving reasons for insisting it be me you married, but you only listed two."

"With many parts."

"None of them really self-serving, however."

"You should tell him," Chuffta counseled. *"It will cost you nothing and will ease things between you."*

"Nothing but my pride," she retorted, but her Familiar only laughed at her. "Should I send for more food? I tasked the hunters to get meat for you, but it will take some time."

"I know—Bero gave me your message." Amusement sparkled from him and he set aside the empty bowl, wiping his hands on the drying cloth and sauntering towards her. "And now I know there's definitely another reason because you're ducking the question."

"You don't know any such thing."

"Oh yes, I do. You change the subject when any of my questions come too close to what you'd prefer to keep hidden."

"That seems impossible for you to keep track of as you ask a great many questions."

"Yes, I do." He nodded, his attention intent on her. "And I'll continue to do so. You might keep your face and body hidden from me, but I'll find other ways to get inside you. Whether you are my enemy or my lover, I'm better off knowing everything about you."

The words, part promise, part threat, made her catch her breath. "I don't have to answer any of your questions. Especially if I'm your enemy."

"Oria." He lifted a hand, as if he might touch her, but hovered it near her cheek, his gaze wandering over her mask, before he lowered it again. "You asked me to be your husband so I can help you with your problems and you can help with mine. The whole point of this effort is to combine forces, to be partners, allies, maybe even friends, if not lovers. There's no reason to treat me like an enemy to be shut out."

"Then why did you say that?"

"To put it out there. We both know we dance a fine line. Let's be clear about it, if only between us."

She closed her eyes, though it didn't help her not see him, feel him in and around her. It was too late to avoid that intimate invasion. Her sgath seemed to flow toward him of its own accord. If only her mother could advise her on this. "The truly self-serving reason is that, if I can't be married to—to have a temple-blessed marriage, then at least I'd be married to someone I…"

"That you what?" he prompted, when she paused too long. He had that avid feel to him, like Chuffta when he hunted.

Pursing her lips and blowing out a breath, she stepped back. "Someone I don't abhor."

He narrowed his eyes. "That's not what you started to

say."

"Well, it's what I decided to say."

"Uh-huh. Do you know that I dreamed about you?"

He had a knack of doing that—disrupting the flow of her thoughts, taking her by surprise, and destabilizing her *hwil*. "No," she replied, face hot under the mask. It was really too steamy in the baths to be wearing it. That and her priestess robes. "Why would I know that?"

"You're a sorceress. I figured one of your magic tricks might be to send me dreams." A bit of tension filled his voice. Enough uncertainty that she decided not to ask what the dreams involved. She'd had plenty of her own about him, and if his were anything like hers…

"No. It most assuredly is not." She folded her hands, then felt too prim, and dropped them. "Now, if we can discuss—"

"If you didn't send them, then I had them because I couldn't get you out of my mind," he interrupted, though his voice was quiet. "I think you were about to say at least you'd be married to someone you're attracted to—and I'm saying I'm attracted to you, too, Oria."

"I know that," she snapped, so thoroughly unsettled that she missed denying that's what she'd been thinking. "I can feel it."

"What does it feel like?" He didn't come closer, but his energy intensified so much that it expanded to flow over her, almost overwhelming. Also addicting, like being warmed by a sun that never burned.

"I just—Lonen—can we please drop this topic and discuss next steps? I've arranged to meet with my mother, to discuss this plan with her. If we're going to go ahead with this, I must go now."

"You have to schedule time with her?"

"She's ... not well. My father's death was very hard on her. Her health is tenuous and my window of opportunity narrow because of it."

His warmth chilled. "We all lost a lot of people we loved."

"I know. Believe me—" She couldn't think about it. Her father dead. Ben and his sweet smile gone forever. Nat. Her lady-in-waiting. Her faithful guard. She couldn't count all the deaths and the misery they'd left in their wakes. "This is another thing that's difficult to explain to an outsider, but my father and mother shared a special bond. Her grief is no greater than anyone's, but losing him caused her ... damage."

Lonen looked thoughtful. "Did they have one of these temple-blessed marriages—ideal mates?"

A warrior of such skill shouldn't be so clever, too. It simply wasn't fair. "Yes," she admitted. "And that's all I'm saying about it."

"That doesn't mean I won't keep asking." He grinned and she realized she'd made a huff of frustration. "Okay, you'll explain your plan to her and then what?"

"If she approves, she'll approach the temple and we can be married as soon as tonight, and begin proceedings with the council to make me queen, in case Yar returns sooner than I expect." And so she could begin her research into the Trom and be ready to wrest control from him.

"I cannot stress enough how much you should not hasten that step, at the peril of not only your sanity, but the wellbeing of us all." Chuffta's mind-voice held unusual sternness, but she ignored him, focusing on convincing Lonen to stop his games and think about the tasks immediately before them.

"And if she doesn't approve?" he was asking.

"Then we'll have to go with the plan of you throwing your weight around. But it would be smoother with her help."

"Makes sense."

"Tomorrow the council meets. I'll petition them to ratify us as king and queen. Once we have the marriage in place, you and I can plan our strategy with the council, if that's all right with you."

"Sounds good." He picked up his axe, the dense iron double-bladed head like a hole in her sgath vision. "Let's go."

"You're … coming with me?"

He grinned at her. "Of course. We're doing this together. Partners. *We* have a fight on our hands—not just you."

"We're not married yet."

"But that's the plan. Which means tonight is our wedding night." That wave of fierce sexuality rolled over her.

"Not in the way you mean."

"We'll figure out something to consummate the momentous occasion. Lead the way, my lovely fiancée."

Setting her teeth against several replies, she did.

LONEN COULDN'T QUITE define to himself why he enjoyed teasing Oria so much. Maybe because it came close—a distant second, but still—to actually touching her. If he couldn't seize her and kiss her breathless, rattling that infernal poise, he could at least make her sound all faint with words.

Besides, it was fun.

For the first time since he'd accepted the king's wreath and the burden of leading the Destrye over his father's corpse, here with Oria he'd gone long minutes without giving any thought to his crushing responsibilities and the looming threat of disaster from so many directions. He couldn't do any more for his people than he was at that moment—which included giving up a normal marriage and very likely the hope of having heirs of his own. He couldn't regret that aspect too deeply. Not as far as his responsibilities to the Destrye were concerned. It would be fitting for Ion's boys to inherit the throne that their father should have had.

That he minded the loss for himself came as something of a surprise. Somewhere deep in his heart he'd nursed the idea that he'd have a loving wife and children to be his family one day. That he wouldn't always feel so alone.

Amazing that any such tender idealism had survived all he'd seen and done.

Dueling with Oria provided a most welcome distraction from such useless thoughts. Also, with every indignant retort and flummoxed response, she became less enigmatic fantasy creature and more flesh and blood woman to him. A welcome transformation. Along with the most pleasant news that he at least hadn't been alone in his strange obsession with her. There might be hope for their marriage yet. It might never be the loving union he'd dreamt of, the wife who'd listen to his foolish thoughts and deepest fears, who he'd be able to confide in when the throne demanded he keep a brave face for all others. But maybe they could make something of a friendship.

If nothing else, conspiring with her to navigate Báran politics was far better than making decisions on his own. He'd never wanted to be king of Destrye. He wouldn't refuse the path Arill set for him, but maybe along with the punishment Oria would be, the goddess also offered him someone to share the trials of that path.

Oria led him out of the baths to a back stairway, walking just ahead of him with spine straight and chin high. Chuffta rode on her shoulder, head swiveling to watch him with those discerning green eyes. Hard to believe such a small skull could contain much intelligence, though he had to admit the Familiar demonstrated more of it than a typical animal, clearly much smarter than his own hunting hounds. The Trom had ridden much larger dragonish creatures that looked much the same as the derkesthai, only in darker colors. Perhaps the adult version of her Familiar. Not a reassuring possibility.

"Is Chuffta a juvenile?" He asked.

"No, he just acts juvenile—hey!" She slapped a hand at Chuffta, freeing the braid he'd yanked with sharp teeth, her giggle like water in the desert. A fascinating woman, so remote, even stern at times, cloaked with magic that shone almost as brightly to his eyes as her copper hair, and then almost girlish in her innocence. She hadn't stepped outside Bára until he forced her to, and she evinced an almost childlike naiveté about the world even a short distance beyond the walls. More than that, she'd told him she mostly stayed in her tower, living alone but for her Familiar and visits from her mother. Why?

"Why?" Oria asked, an uncanny echo of his thoughts. It took him moment to think back.

"I thought maybe Chuffta would grow into one of those dragon creatures the Trom flew in on." Chuffta's mouth parted, showing sharply fanged teeth, long forked tongue lolling out, for all the world looking like a ferocious smile.

Apparently Oria didn't perceive *that* because she continued walking, smoothly replying, "He says not, though I wondered the same thing. He told me that would be like comparing a house cat to one of the golden desert jaguars." She breathed a laugh. "Also he wants me to tell you that he's far smarter than the Trom dragons, who he calls vile and witless beasts." At the top of the stairwell, she turned and followed a narrow interior hall, stuffy from the lack of windows that normally graced most Báran passageways.

"Is this a servants' corridor?"

"Yes." She glanced back at him, an odd habit as she clearly didn't need to. Perhaps because she hadn't had her mask long. "I hope you're not offended. I mean no insult, only to hide your presence in Bára as long as possible."

His hands twitched with the impulse to slide around her waist and pull her back against him, to kiss that delectably exposed nape and tease her about offending him. Could he really never touch her at all? If skin-to-skin contact was the problem, perhaps he could wear gloves... He had some for cold weather—unfortunately back in Dru. "No, I'm not at all offended. The Destrye are not like your Báran men, so obsessed with status. I ask out of simple curiosity."

"You seem to have plenty of that and none of it simple," she muttered, then stopped before a door, rapping on it briskly, then opening it. "Would you make sure she's alone?"

Lonen took a step to oblige, but Chuffta spread his wide white wings and took off from her shoulder, doing his mistress's bidding—much as Lonen himself had been so eager to do. Ion would be laughing his ass off. *Don't let a bit of foreign pussy make you think with the little head instead of the big one.* For once the memory of his eldest brother didn't come with a wave of fresh grief. If he watched from the Hall of Warriors, Ion would be hugely amused that Lonen had not only failed to follow what was likely very good advice, but wouldn't even enjoy the promised reward for his loss of good sense.

"All right, let's go in," Oria said suddenly, her voice and body tense. She'd probably overheard his salacious thought. Maybe she could teach him how to keep his more obnoxious fantasies hidden. It didn't seem like she heard *everything* that crossed his mind—maybe mainly the ones he was more enthusiastic about.

"Ready?" she prompted, looking back at him, something in her voice. Maybe it wasn't that he provoked her, but her own nerves over presenting her plan to this former queen Lonen had never glimpsed.

"Do I look all right?" he asked her, partly to tease, but also to give her a moment to recover her poise. "I wouldn't want to bias your mother against her future son-in-law by looking like I fell out of a tree."

Oria tilted her head slightly, facing him. She'd be wrinkling the bridge of her nose for his frivolity. "You have"—she waved fingers at his temple—"some hair that's come loose."

"Where?"

She pointed. "Right there."

Deliberately he stroked a hand over the wrong spot. "I don't feel anything."

Chuffta flew back, landing on her shoulder, and she huffed her impatience. "Really it's not important and she's waiting for us."

"Can't you fix it for me?"

"No," she drew out the word as if he might be stupid after all. "Because I can't touch you."

"You said skin to skin—this is skin to hair. They're different."

"Lonen." She put her hands on her hips, bristling with exasperation.

"Just try," he coaxed. "You said your mother's good opinion and support are important."

"You don't know that," she said in a sharp tone.

"Excuse me?"

"Not you." She waved a hand to erase the words. "I'm sorry. I was replying to Chuffta. It's not always easy with both of you talking at me at once."

He and the derkesthai exchanged rueful looks, an odd brotherhood. "He thinks you can try?"

"Yes." She sighed her exasperation. "Fine. But don't move."

He could swear her Familiar gave him a knowing nod of complicity before leaning his cheek against the smooth skin under Oria's ear. She relaxed at the contact—deriving some kind of stability or comfort from it—and stepped closer to him. With slowly tentative fingers, she reached up, caught the escaped curls, and tucked them back in with deft skill.

That close, her heady scent of lilies wafted over him and he imagined her face intent as she took care not to touch him. "Are you all right?" he asked her quietly and she stilled, her copper eyes perhaps flying to his.

"So far," she breathed, the outline of her exquisite breasts rising and falling under the silk. Though he'd called the robe shapeless and ugly, in truth it clung in exactly the right places, even if it did cover up too much. She stepped back abruptly, erecting that chill barrier between them again. "No more delays. And let me do the talking."

Happy enough with the results of that test, he bowed and gestured for her to precede him, though he reserved the right to speak up if necessary. She pivoted, her tiny behind twitching as she stalked away into a set of rooms that exceeded even his imaginings for the former queen of Bára. Sculptures made of more glass twined in shades of ice-white, gold, and rose, scattered about the room. The floor of mosaicked tiles reflected light like the treacherous ice cliffs in the sea off Dru. All of it had a cooling effect—soothing in the desert climate, perhaps—but he found he preferred Oria's sunny and lush rooftop terrace, with the vivid sails of silk catching the breezes and her fire table of violet flames.

Elegant even by Báran standards, the lavishly furnished and decorated chambers looked out through grand arched windows to the city wall just below—though across the deep chasm that divided the palace grounds from the city proper—and then to the wide, desolate plain and distant hills beyond. When he wasn't baking in the landscape, Lonen could appreciate its austere appeal, the clean, simple lines and radiant colors reminding him of Oria.

All thoughts led back to Oria. His particular goddess and doom.

This, then, was the window he'd glimpsed her in that night, as he'd run along that very wall. Now, as then, her Familiar took a perch upon the sill, green eyes knowing.

A woman rose from a chair by that window, dressed more richly than the common women who strolled the paths of Bára, but not in the crimson priestess robes or even as grandly as Oria had for state occasions on his previous visit. She also wore no mask, her eyes a deep enough brown to contrast with her golden hair, but neither as spectacular a color as Oria's. Their kinship shone clear, however, in the widely set eyes framed by delicate brows and arched cheekbones, fine lines accenting her fair skin, and in her slight, willowy build. She looked as his wife would decades from now, a strange glimpse of the future. If he ever saw Oria's face again.

The intensity of her gaze had Lonen forcing himself to continue forward, despite the uncanny prickling of his scalp. Had his neck not been freshly shaved, those hairs would be standing up, too.

"What is this about, Oria?" The woman's eyes flashed with

hatred that seemed to crawl across his skin like fireants, but she drew her daughter into a gentle embrace, holding her a moment before releasing her and facing Lonen. Without waiting for Oria's explanation, she launched her attack. "Destrye. I can't imagine what brings you back to Bára—surely you've pillaged enough. We have nothing more to sacrifice to your bloodthirsty lusts."

If she only knew about those lusts.

"Mother," Oria inserted herself between them. "You did not have the opportunity to meet before. This is King Lonen of the Destrye—not the king who led their armies to Bára. He's a good man and an honorable ruler, doing his best as we are, to salvage something for the future from this terrible conflict. He's come here in peace, to ask for our help."

A pretty speech and not entirely accurate—as he was far from good and honorable—but he wouldn't object even silently as Oria calling him that made up for any bending of the truth. He did send a mental apology to his father, however, for not defending his honor. As the former queen's hard gaze came back to him, he tried to look like a good and honorable king, and not a giddy lad flattered by a pretty girl's sweet words.

"King Lonen"—Oria inclined her head—"my mother, Rihanna, former queen and priestess of Bára."

No title for the woman now, apparently, but he bowed to her anyway. "I greet you, lady mother of Bára, and thank you for your hospitality under such trying circumstances."

"What do you want of us?" The former queen's face remained still and remote as a carved statue, but her dark eyes held dread. "We have nothing left to give."

"Mother." Oria took her mother's hands, skin to skin, Lonen noted. So it could be done. "The Trom have attacked

Dru and again stolen water."

Though pale as ice already, the former queen blanched, then eased herself into a chair. "Oh, Yar," she whispered.

"It has to be." Oria went with her, keeping her hand and kneeling at her mother's knee. "There's only one path left to us. I must become queen as soon as possible, both to hold the throne against him and find a way to … take control myself."

Oria didn't look his way, but her mother did, gaze flicking to ascertain how much he understood. "Yourself? You can't mean you propose to try to summon *them*?"

"I do. I see no other way. As queen, I'll have access to all the temple secrets. I have to try this."

"And if you break?" Cagily, Oria's mother looked at him and away again. "We need to discuss your plan without this barbarian present."

"I've proposed to King Lonen that we wed," Oria interrupted. "And he's agreed. If you'll support my choice with the temple we can marry tonight and petition the council tomorrow."

The former queen's expression didn't falter from its smooth serenity, but Lonen didn't miss how her knuckles whitened as she gripped Oria's hands. "This extremity is not what I had in mind when we discussed the necessity of a marriage for you, my daughter." The words seemed to hold a wealth of subtext, enough to fuel a furious urge in him to lay about with his axe and cut through all the stultifying politics. They discussed marriage to him, not a death sentence, though you wouldn't know it from the former queen's dire expression.

"I know what I'm doing."

The former queen shook her head. "I don't know that you do. Are you doing this out of some misplaced guilt?"

Oria's slim shoulders moved in a shimmy of discomfort. "It

seems someone here should be shouldering that very well placed guilt."

"Becoming my honored wife and queen of the Destrye is hardly a punishment," Lonen grated out, harshly enough to startle both women out of their communion.

Oria stood hastily and brushed a slim hand over her immaculate braids, as if caught with a hair out of place. "My apologies, King Lonen. We intended no insult. I am indeed honored to wed you and become your queen, as Bára is privileged to claim you as king."

A pretty speech—she was good at those—but her mother's mouth tightened over unspoken words. "This is why we should discuss this in private, Oria." She raised meaningful brows.

"No." Oria straightened her shoulders and moved to align herself beside him. Not touching him, naturally, but close enough that he could if he forgot himself and tried. "King Lonen is part of this. He's aware that some temple mysteries will remain secrets from him, so speak as you will."

"Is that so?" Rhianna gestured at him with a languid hand, but her eyes bored into him dark and hard as a rare moonless winter night. "Then is he *aware* that he can never bed you? Their barbarian race thinks nothing of rape."

Oria moved slightly in front of him at his growl, forestalling his retort. "We've discussed it. Barbarians they may be, but the Destrye are also a race of disciplined warriors. He will not harm me. He has agreed to a marriage in name only."

"Until he loses self-control." Rhianna's gaze bored into him, as if he'd already defiled her daughter in truth, rather than only in fantasy. "You are innocent of many of the harsher realities of the world outside our walls, Oria. You cannot risk this. Not for any reason."

"The Destrye have a long and bloody history, it's true," Lonen told her, unwilling to remain silent on the topic any longer. "As do your people—something I'm sure must be as well-documented in your texts as in ours. We also have a tradition of protecting women, who are sacred to the goddess Arill. I would allow no one to harm my wife—not even myself."

Oria didn't turn his way, but something about the softening of her posture made him think she paid close attention. Perhaps she mentally read the truth in his words, so he strengthened that sentiment, pushing it towards her.

"Protecting women?" Rhianna's lip curled, emotion cracking her visage. "Is that why you murdered defenseless priestesses in cold blood, one after another, like the animals you slaughter without care?"

Lonen didn't physically flinch, but only through dint of great will. That night, the first priestess he'd killed—the way her wondering eyes went dark with death—had reminded him of the first doe he'd shot. Murder. Yes, it had felt that way, had gone against everything he believed in. Nothing like the fair fight of the battlefield. He'd done it out of extremity, yes, but how to defend an indefensible act?

"I am—"

"You don't deserve a treasure like my daughter," Rhianna spat. "You have no idea what she proposes to do and worse, you mind-dead brute, you won't be able to help her when she needs it most. You'll destroy her instead, like the monster you are."

~ 5 ~

STRUCK HARD BY the wave of guilt and remorse from Lonen—along with a vivid memory image of a dying doe and blood on his hands—and with surprising, strong protective feelings of her own, Oria wrestled the potent emotions. He'd meant every word of what he'd said about not harming her, and about holding the female sacred—a fascinating and foreign image in his mind of a fertile goddess bestowing blessings. The truth resonated in him regardless of the rest.

She deeply regretted bringing him to this meeting.

Once a model of *hwil*, the former queen had become like the bay beyond Bára, her emotional state as unpredictable as the bore tides, and as lethal in their ability to swamp the unwary.

"Enough, Mother," Oria said, venting some of the emotional tension with some judicious grien that took the form of a dust devil swirling past the window, briefly whipping the sheer silk curtains that hung limply by the sides. "We've all committed grave sins in the name of war. You and I may not have held the knife blades, but we've drunk the water bought with the blood of Destrye children. Something you confessed you knew was happening and that you did nothing to stop. None of us are innocent."

She caught a flash of surprised gratitude from Lonen, glad

then that she'd stood up for him in that rare moment of weakness. He seemed so strong, so fierce—even brutal in his anger at times—but he possessed a tender heart under that muscled chest.

"Something you detected in him all along, hmm?"

Ignoring Chuffta's too-smug observation, she forged on. "You've left this to me, Mother. Unless you wish to reclaim your mask and your crown, in which case I'll gladly step aside for you, I need you to support me in this decision."

"So much of this is my fault, the result of my many failures to act..." The former queen nearly chanted the words, sounding like those prematurely aged out of sanity. Oria put a finger to her temple, in lieu of putting her face in her hands. Sometimes her mother seemed like her old self, her mind as incisive as ever, then suddenly...

Lonen brushed the sleeve of her robe, carefully not touching her skin, but putting her on alert regardless. He had an inquiring feel to him and an image formed of a person tending to her mother. Was he silently asking if the former queen needed a healer? She shook her head minutely, just in case. Her mother was beyond help.

"Then don't fail to act now." She said it crisply, as her mother might once have prodded her, adding a nudge of grien. "You promised to help me. This is how you can. I need you to do this."

Rhianna lifted a tear-streaked face, her sgath hanging about her like tattered rags. "I wanted so much more for you, my beautiful and powerful daughter. You should have an ideal match, a man who will treasure you and know you as you deserve to be known, give life to your magic, bring you wealth and glory, and provide you children. No one less than the most powerful of Báran kings deserves you, not this mind-dead—"

"Will you intervene with the temple or not?" Oria cut her off as she should have done much earlier. No anger wafted off Lonen, however—at least, not more than the dark, brooding fury that seemed to underlie most of his thoughts. Had he always been of that nature or had the war done that to him? An intensely curious interest prowled over her that tasted distinctly of him. No doubt he'd have more questions for her. Joy.

Then disappointment crushed her relatively minor aggravation.

"I won't do it." Her mother lifted her chin, an echo of the proud queen she'd been. "I won't cooperate in sending you to your doom. Not even to save Bára. The sacrifice is too great."

"This is my marriage, my decision, my life."

"Don't ask me to help you ruin it. I love you too much." Her mother fulminated with dark sgath, much of it reaching towards Lonen like the shadowy tentacles of the wyrms that lurked in the damp cellars of Bára. Time to get him away from her. No telling what her unstable magic could do, even as passively as sgath typically worked. Oria had seen her mother blur those lines, too.

She set her teeth, keeping the flawless façade of *hwil*. "I won't ask it then. But I will marry him and petition the council for the crown tomorrow. Will you support me then?"

Rhianna turned her face to the window, face once again remote, seeing only the past. "I am not well." Her voice wobbled and she swallowed hard.

"I know, Mother." Oria's heart thudded dully with the pain of seeing her like this. For a while it had seemed she'd recover, but lately she only seemed to fall further into the depths of her mind, her sanity fracturing more with every descent. "Don't fret. I'll visit you in the morning and we can talk."

Her mother didn't reply, so Oria beckoned to Chuffta, who flew to her shoulder. The winding of his long tail around her arm gave her comfort.

"It was a bad day. Perhaps she'll be more lucid tomorrow," he said as they withdrew. Lonen paced stoically at her side, his emotions tightly reined, thoughts unusually opaque.

"She was lucid enough for a while there—enough to recognize what a terrible idea this is."

"I don't think it's a terrible idea."

"You don't?" Her toe caught the hem of her robe in her moment of inattention. *"But you said that—"*

"That the Destrye king would not be easily led. I think he is a good mate for you."

She rolled her eyes behind the mask. *"Like you'd know."*

He gave her the mental equivalent of a shrug. *"You like him. The rest can be overcome."*

"Now you sound like him."

"Attempting to summon the Trom yourself, however," he continued, turning severe, *"that is a terrible idea. Even your mother retains enough wit to know that. You run the risk of—"*

She bumped her shoulder to interrupt the lecture, making her Familiar spread his wings for balance. *"I'm not discussing this right now."*

"You could be having this conversation with me, you know," Lonen commented.

They emerged into the servants' corridor and Oria paused, both undecided about the direction they should take and chagrined at Lonen's remark. "I apologize." She made herself face him. "I'm in the habit of being with Chuffta and talking to him, not with…"

"Another human being?" he supplied, a ripple of humor beneath it.

Why that made her blush, she had no idea. His body heat, perhaps, like a coal brazier in the narrow, enclosed hall. "Right," she replied, determined to leave it at that.

"What happened to her?" Lonen asked, with so much gentle concern it nearly undid her.

"I explained already. My father's death damaged her."

"You said because of this ideal mate business."

"Yes." She braced herself for a barrage of more questions.

He pondered, however, hand stroking thoughtfully over his beard. "It seems to me that if I make guesses, then you're not technically telling me secrets."

"Lonen…" She hated the helpless sound in her voice, but she didn't know what she could possibly say to explain any of it. The encounter with her damaged mother had left her wrung dry and facing High Priestess Febe felt beyond her. They should go to the temple and do that next, but she couldn't quite find the impetus to leave the stuffy, shadowed corridor. Perhaps all of it had been a stupid, hopeless plan. She was so tired of fighting.

"Give me some rope here and see if I can climb on my own." Lonen leaned against the wall and crossed his ankles, still stroking his beard as he studied her. She didn't object because at least she could hide a little longer. "Your mother called me 'mind-dead,' which I assume refers to my not being a sorcerer."

"I'm really sorry about that," she whispered in furious embarrassment. "She's—"

"You apologize too much. I'm not offended, though I gather that's an insult. I know as well as you do that I don't have magic. I don't consider this a failing. I don't want it, except maybe to help build aqueducts."

Bemused, she parsed the word. "Build what?"

"Never mind. An idle thought, and something we can discuss later, when you come with me to Dru."

"Which I can't promise that—"

"Yes, yes, I know. Never mind that, either. What's important at the moment is that I gather that is this ideal mate thing would connect you mentally to your husband, and there's some sort of magical component, too. Which your mother and father had and she's distressed to the point of refusing to help you marry me because she places such a high value on wanting that for you."

"It's not really that—"

"'The sacrifice is too great'—her exact words."

"Stop interrupting me!" She nearly stamped her foot with the frustration at both the Destrye and Chuffta snickering in her head.

"Then stop saying things that don't matter," he fired back, shocking her. "This is an important conversation."

"That we're having in a servant's corridor," she pointed out.

He chuckled at that, that welcome sunny humor of his dispersing some of her emotional gloom. "When we celebrate our two decades' anniversary, we can recapitulate this day and meet each other entirely in baths and hallways."

"We did talk on my rooftop terrace earlier, as well, when I proposed marriage." Which seemed like days ago, not hours.

"Good point. I'm adding rooftop terraces to the list, though if we're in Dru we might have to substitute a tree-house."

"A house in a tree?" Something that had never occurred to her, partly because she'd never seen a tree big enough to hold an entire house. But the image in his head showed a forest of enormous trees, the leaves so dense they blocked the sun, and a structure of wood in the crux of a network of branches. The image changed so it seemed she stood inside it, looking out, the forest floor as far below as the streets of Bára from her terrace. It struck her that he'd changed the 'view' deliberately, to show her another angle.

"Are you doing that on purpose?"

"What—picturing things for you to see in my mind? Yeah. I figure if you're going to read my thoughts anyway, I might as well take advantage of it. It could be a handy secret weapon for us."

A laugh escaped her, lessening the tightness of grief and despair. "You're unlike anyone I've ever known."

"Good." He grinned, but under it a surge of possessive lust intensified the simple approval. "As I'm the only husband you'll ever have, mind-dead and unable to give life to your magic as I might be, I'll have to make it up in other ways."

"I'm really sorry she said those things."

"Another apology, and for something you can't control. I don't mind, Oria." He pushed off the wall and it seemed he might reach for her, but he stopped himself. "I'd much rather know the unvarnished truth of how it will be between us. No secrets to fester. If you're making a grave sacrifice by marrying me—one I approve of as it will save both our peoples—then I want to know exactly what you're giving up, so I can do what I can to compensate for it. I'd like to think I can offer you some happiness, if not exactly what you were expecting."

"Oh." The corridor was too hot. That was why she felt a little faint.

"Your mother is wrong." Lonen sounded gravely determined, that warrior's resolve enfolding her, an image in his mind of him taking her in a gentle embrace that very nearly felt real. "I will treasure you, Oria, and I'll do my best to know you, but you have to let me in."

"I don't need that. That's not why we're doing this."

"I need it." His emotions, complex and shifting with layers, intensified.

"But why?"

He shrugged, impatient with the question, but continued to refine the image of holding her in his mind. "Maybe I've had plenty of misery, too much blood and loss and death. We might be marrying for political reasons, but that doesn't mean we can't bring something bright to each other's lives. That we can't take care of each other." The sense of his arms around her made it almost believable.

"How are you doing that?"

"If you sense how I feel, what's in my head, then I can give you this much. If I can't hold you and comfort you, then there's this, yes?"

"The Destrye is wiser than he seems at first."

Oria didn't know what to do with Chuffta's seemingly sudden and enthusiastic approval of Lonen, so she ignored him.

"I know it hurt you to see your mother that way," Lonen continued in a gentle tone. "It would be painful for anyone. My father, King Archimago, when my brother Nolan fell into a crevasse on the battlefield… in some ways he never recovered from that."

"I'm sorry," she whispered.

"Stop," he replied, but with a kind of tenderness. "As you said in there, we've all done things. I've done things I'll carry the stain of to my grave. But what I'm trying to tell you is that if your mother is in this state because her ideal mate died, then perhaps it will be a strength for you, that you won't be exposed to that danger with me."

She lifted her head in surprise, amazed at the way his masculine vitality had filled the narrow space, embracing her, weaving in with her sgath. "I'd never thought of it that way."

"See?" He was all smug male then. "You can learn things from me, too."

She huffed at him, not even caring that it made him grin. "I'm not convinced of that, Destrye."

"That's all right. I'll be convinced for both of us." He lifted a hand, moving close enough to trace the fall of one of her braids, though he kept a whisper distance from it. His granite-colored eyes seemed silver bright viewed with her sgath, like the white-hot heart of a glass forge. "Maybe I should be sorry that I won't be the husband you deserve, but I'm not. I'd hate to see you like that, with your fire dimmed and your sharp mind dulled."

"She used to be so much more."

"I saw glimpses of it. She must have been a formidable woman and queen. I regret I didn't meet her before."

"We all carry regrets," Oria echoed his earlier words. "And I, for one, am tired of wallowing in them. You're right—you and I are about moving forward. No more apologies, yes?"

"Works for me."

The moment felt oddly intimate. So much so that she moved away, putting safer distance between them. "I suppose that moving forward means going to the temple and convincing High Priestess Febe to marry us."

"Time for the strategy that Bára and everything in it, including you, belongs to me?" Lonen's energy took on a feral, sharp edge—one that strangely put her in mind of the iron axe he carried on his back.

"As a gambit only," she told him, bringing her own mettle to it. "Don't go getting the wrong idea about me."

He only nodded and gestured for her to lead the way. "This time, you'll leave the talking to me."

~ 6 ~

ORIA REMAINED SUBDUED, but seemed less crushed than when they'd left her mother's chambers. Lonen congratulated himself for both distracting her from her troubles and also making inroads on earning her trust. Her secrets would not become like the fanged and clawed Báran golems, tearing at their entrails until they resented each other rather than rightfully hating the pain instead. As he had with the golems, he'd hunt those secrets down, one by one, and destroy them. His iron axe cut through the magical creatures; he could cleave her magical secrets into dust as well.

Once he'd ferreted them out. Including the one her mother had alluded to: *And if you break?* Something about Oria's plan worried him—and had upset her mother, too. He'd thought no price would be too high to pay to save the Destrye, but… No. What was he thinking? His first loyalty belonged to his people. No matter his other interests in Oria, his softer regard toward her—all of that fell into the same set of considerations as his own happiness. They'd both do whatever it took for the greater good.

But he *would* find out what she faced, and what the stakes would be.

He listened as Oria explained in hushed tones how the temple hierarchy worked and the path they'd take to where the High Priestess would receive them. As soon as they emerged from the servants' corridor, word of his presence in Bára would fly ahead of them, faster than jewelbirds.

"What are jewelbirds?"

He got the impression she rolled her eyes at him, considering the question irrelevant. "I'll show you one, in my garden. They're small, fast and beautiful—they come to the flowers."

The flowers that died inch by inch without water under the scorching sun. Another thing Oria loved that would be lost to her. Nothing compared to what the Destrye had lost, but it bothered him still.

They arrived at a small waiting chamber and she sent a guard to bring her a substantial escort. There would be no surprising the High Priestess, she'd explained, so they might as well take the public halls. At that point, the more people who knew what was going on, the better. She seemed to believe the people would support her. From what he'd seen when she'd offered the city's surrender, he agreed.

Though privately he thought they'd love her better without the mask and crimson robes of the very temple they all so clearly feared.

"And your role in this battle?" he asked. "Will you be the frightened virgin terrorized into marrying her conqueror?"

She actually laughed, a lighthearted musical sound, however brief. "While I'm largely regarded as fragile, none of the priestesses would believe I could be terrorized, even by a man as intimidating as you. I shall play the nobly resigned daughter of the house of Tavlor and Rhianna. With luck, Febe will be so pleased to see me brought low and consigned to a mind-dead marriage, she'll agree to your demands for that reason alone."

"You find me intimidating?" The concept both startled him and made him absurdly proud. And here he'd thought Oria the one with all the power in her slim, magical hands.

"I can't believe that's what you focused on from everything I said."

He went to an unglassed window that overlooked one of the yawning chasms that cracked through Bára, making her towers seem that much taller by comparison. It probably didn't speak well of him that it salved his pride to know she found him intimidating, especially as it wouldn't necessarily contribute to happy relations between them. "What about me intimidates you?"

"You're big." She said it with a shrug in her voice. "And you carry a great big battle-axe that could chop me into little wriggly bits."

Wriggly bits. The more he came to know her, the more he glimpsed what might be a playful, even whimsical personality. And perhaps much of her bravery came from a rash disregard for her own wellbeing. Which brought him right back to whatever foolhardy plan she entertained.

"What did your mother mean about you 'breaking' if you try to summon the Trom? What magic is involved there?" He watched her carefully, so he caught how she stiffened defensively, lacing her fingers together as if that might hide from him what she planned.

"That's nothing I can explain to you." *Destrye.* She didn't say it aloud, but the haughty tone conveyed the slamming of temple doors against the outsider.

"Can't or won't?" he growled back. If she put him in mind of a housecat, all fluff and hiss, then he'd meet her posture for posture.

She inclined her head regally. "They are functionally the same. And regardless, this place is not private enough to discuss the situation, even if I could. It's best for you not to mention the Trom or my magic at all. I can hardly trust you with my secrets if you insist on discussing them indiscreetly. Don't worry about the magical aspects of this plan, King Lonen, I'll see to my end of the bargain."

He set his teeth against his irritation. "At what cost to you?"

"What's it to you?" she fired back. "Enough with this protective and solicitous charade you've adopted. Expiate your guilt some other way. Yes, you killed our priestesses and no, you didn't want to. But you can't bring them back by saving me any more than you can resurrect that poor doe whose throat you cut because your arrow missed her heart."

The sally struck his own heart, thudding into the old wound with painful accuracy. "I shouldn't be surprised you saw that in my head, but it's harsh and cold of you to use that against me. If my size and axe intimidate you, then just imagine what it's like for me to have you prowling about in my secret soul, unearthing pains no one would know about otherwise."

She lifted a hand to Chuffta, stroking him for her own comfort, he surmised, a tremor in the gesture. "I know you told me not to apologize anymore, but I'm offering one anyway. My abilities are ... new to me and somewhat ungovernable. I've also spent little time around people and you—well, I don't mean to see these things. But you're right that it was wrong to try to hurt you with that information."

"Is that what you were doing?" He studied her, the tense lines of her shoulders making the silk robe look as if it hung on hooks, not soft flesh. "I think that whatever you're planning is dangerous, and you don't like anyone pointing that out to you."

Chuffta fixed him with a gimlet green stare and Lonen

could swear the Familiar practically nodded at him.

For her part, Oria had curled her fingers into tiny fists. "My goal is to help *your* people. That's why you came to me and that's the reason we're doing all of this. You have your part; I have mine. Don't you dare question how I intend to go about it."

"You mean, how you go about expiating your own guilt?" His taunt, throwing her words back at her, hit home he was sure, but she barely showed it.

"Don't pretend to know me, Destrye," she said softly, with surprising menace. Her magic curled around him, a palpable thing. The sensation might once have revolted him, but it had become part of being in Oria's presence, along with her scent and beguiling figure. Perversely, he even liked that she threatened him. She had that much correct—no one would believe her as the terrified virgin.

But he did come to know her. In time, he would know her even more. Once he'd bound her to him in marriage, she'd have no escape. Threaten as she might, she would never actually harm him, no more than he'd take his axe to her. He snorted out a laugh, making her turn from her restless pacing.

"You laugh?" she hissed.

"Wriggly bits, indeed," he replied, shaking his head.

It made her pause, and then her escort of armed City Guard arrived to escort them to the temple, ending further argument between them.

They walked side by side, the guard flanking and following, deeper into the palace than he'd been before. As with all of Bára, the halls were open and spacious, with regular windows open to the breezes that relieved the intense heat of afternoon. As Oria had predicted, people noted his presence with variations of shock and alarm, any number of young servants and the occasional crimson-robe figure dashing off to spread the news. He imagined them like Oria's jewelbirds, zooming about from flower to flower.

They emerged from the far side of the public areas of the palace and onto a bridge that spanned a smaller chasm to yet another set of towers, built entirely of rose-colored stone carved in circles, tiled with blue-white moons in various phases. A tribute to the moons Sgatha and Grienon.

At the far end of the short span, the high priestess stood flanked by two priests. Though they all wore the smooth golden masks of their office, the high priestess had become familiar to him with her extravagantly braided white hair, and the priests recognizable as male by their bulk. Such as it was— the Báran men stood taller than Oria, but generally slight in stature compared to Destrye warriors. Even starved and overworked, Lonen likely outweighed these men by half again.

No wonder Oria found him physically intimidating. Yet another way he'd never be the husband she'd expected to have, in yet another aspect totally out of his control.

"Destrye." The High Priestess's voice rang like a hollow gong. "You are not allowed within the sacred temple of Bára. Princess Oria, what is the meaning of this intrusion?"

"High Priestess, I—"

Without thinking, Lonen grasped Oria's upper arm, stopping her and asserting his command of the situation. This, he *could* control. She stiffened with a gasp, but Chuffta didn't leap to her defense, so it seemed his touch over the robe didn't harm her, or at least not overly much. Nevertheless, he loosened his grip.

"You will address me as Your Highness," he informed the High Priestess in a cool tone that should convey both his rank and her trespass. "Or King Lonen. I'm here to invoke the ancient right of conqueror. I claim Princess Oria as mine. You will bind her to me under your laws."

Oria had gone quiet and still, barely breathing, and he would have given a great deal at that moment for her trick of reading thoughts and emotions. High Priestess Febe betrayed nothing of her reaction, but the sense of magic thickened. Nothing like battles with mages to teach a warrior to pay attention to impending attack of an uncanny nature. Magic built much like static charges in still air heralded a bolt of lightning. The wise man took cover in such circumstances.

If only he could.

He shook Oria's arm, trying to make it look forceful without requiring a tighter grip. "Command them to stand down. You've acknowledged my claim as lawful—and you've been warned of the consequences should your people attempt to do me harm."

"It's true," she blurted, her voice strained. Concerned that he might be hurting her through the thin silk, he let go under guise of thrusting her forward. She stumbled slightly on the too-long hem of her robes, but caught herself, straightening proudly. *Nobly resigned daughter of the house of Tavlor and Rhianna.* He had to force back the smile, concentrating on his deep well of anger, although the rage didn't leap to mind as eagerly as usual.

"The Destrye king has returned to claim me as his. He's willing to make me his wife under Báran law." Oria managed to sound infuriated, frightened, courageous, and forbearing all at once. Quite the woman, his Báran sorceress. "His armies wait beyond the bay, as a token of good faith, but if he does not signal them at set intervals, they will invade Bára and this time they won't leave again."

Febe surveyed him, taking her time, but a flick of her fingers had the sense of impending lightning dispersing. "How has King Lonen entered the city without my knowledge? His Highness wears the clothes of a Báran man, so it appears he's been here long enough to be tended."

"Your knowledge?" Oria's tone went scathing. "I'm unaware of a change in protocol that would have the City Guard notifying the temple of a high-ranking visitor before the royal family."

"Indeed, High Priestess Febe," Captain Ercole, a stalwart and canny soldier who'd led the resistance against the Destrye and won Lonen's respect as few Báran fighters had, stepped forward. "King Lonen arrived and requested an immediate audience with the ruling family. With Prince Yar out of the city and the former queen Rhianna unable to receive visitors, I escorted him to Princess Oria. Our scouts have verified the presence of his armies on the far side of the bay," he added smoothly, as if they'd practiced the deception. Lonen appreciated Oria's cleverness in protecting him. In retrospect, bringing an army—or even a small guard—would have been smarter. Arnon had argued viciously for it. But Lonen had been unwilling to lead yet more Destrye into conflict and possible death. That reluctance might prove to be his great failing as a king. Or one of them. So many to choose from.

"Why now, Your Highness?" Febe turned her attention to him, her manner more obsequious. "We thought you satisfied with the treaty you made and required nothing more of Bára. Certainly not her most treasured daughter."

He allowed himself to smile, ever so slightly. If they shared Oria's abilities they would sense something of his emotions. So he allowed the feelings of lust and possessiveness—even obsession—for Oria to rise up. With a careful hand he picked up one of her long, perfectly plaited braids, running it through his fingers. It glinted in the sunlight like finely wrought copper chain. "I discovered I could not forget a certain Báran princess. The Destrye have a long, much celebrated history of taking women from Bára and your sister cities to serve us. It occurred to me that with the defeat of Bára, it's time to resurrect the tradition. A trophy, if you will, as lasting memory of our triumph and your defeat."

"Our Trom bloodied you and yours, Your Highness. But for Princess Oria's concessions to you, Bára might have called it your defeat."

"Is that so?" He made it sound bored, the texture of Oria's hair finer than silk, his fingers itching to unplait it all and run his fingers through the coppery shimmer of it. As he'd hoped, it seemed she easily tolerated his touch to her hair, her breathing quiet and Chuffta peaceful. "Perhaps you need another demonstration of Destrye might. Call your Trom and drive us out again if you can."

One of the priests murmured to Febe, his mask inclined towards hers, and she turned away with some irritation. Good thing that Oria had told him their threats would be empty with Yar away from the city.

"Perhaps it need not come to that, Your Highness," Febe spread her hands, all accommodation. "The temple acknowledges your right as conqueror to claim a woman of Bára, and we accept that it is Princess Oria who has seized your attention. But you need not marry her. If you wish to take her away, back to your homeland, we will be unable to prevent you. We ask only that you take her and go in peace, without troubling the people of Bára further."

~ 7 ~

THE TRAITOROUS BITCH. Of course she should have realized High Priestess Febe would seize the opportunity to be rid of Oria and her unknown potential that bothered the other woman so. *Ponen*, the Trom had called her. At least Oria had accurately predicted that the priestess would be pleased to see Oria consigned to such a terrible fate—indeed, smug delight radiated through the woman's *hwil*, with hints of stronger, darker emotions beneath—but she'd miscalculated the depth of the high priestess's ambition and disregard for Oria's wellbeing. She'd cheerfully send Oria off to be a sex slave to the Destrye king, knowing full well how quickly it would kill her, never mind the rest. With not even slim protection a temple marriage would afford her.

She scrambled to think of a way to persuade Febe that marriage would be necessary, but Lonen was, again, ahead of her. Fortunate, as his gentle caress on her braid sent distracting heat through her. And not of the painful, distressing variety. Seductive and soothing at the same time, the sensation made her want to lean into him for more. A very bad idea as it would turn destructive in the blink of an eye.

"You think me unworthy of marrying a Báran princess, High Priestess?" Lonen was saying, his voice as dark and edged with violence as the anger fulminating at the forefront of his mind. At that moment he seemed every bit as ruthless and terrifying as the illustrations of his Destrye ancestors, delighting as they burned and pillaged. "I don't propose to help myself to a random assortment of Bára's wealth—though that idea holds appeal, also—I want Princess Oria as my bride, forever cementing that Bára belongs to Dru. She'll be my queen and I shall be King of Bára."

Febe didn't quite look to Oria, but her smugness had gone carefully avaricious. "Is this agreeable to you, Princess Oria? We all know what you'd be sacrificing, taking the Destrye king as your husband. Bára would hate to see you leave her walls forever. It's unfortunate His Highness is so impatient, or we'd await Prince Yar's return, so he could witness the ritual."

A strategically worded message—that still managed to avoid acknowledging that the high priestess would send Oria to a short life of sexual servitude that would eventually kill her. If going outside the walls didn't take care of that sooner rather than later. Febe knew perfectly well that Lonen marrying Oria wouldn't automatically make him King of Bára. Her mistake, however, was in believing Oria would be in collusion with her to mislead him—and that Yar would inevitably return with an ideal bride to put paid to the Destrye's ambitions. Febe might be thinking that Lonen and Oria would be long gone by the time Yar returned, in which case Lonen's assumption that he was King of Bára would last awhile with no information to contradict that belief. In the scenario Febe likely envisioned, he might labor under that misapprehension far longer than Oria would survive.

"Like my mother and father before me, I'm bred to my duty to Bára," Oria replied, holding to her role of resignation to her terrible fate to yet again save her city, all handled with a demonstrable exercise of *hwil*. Febe thought her a fool for it, but then she'd never contemplate making any sort of sacrifice, much less of the level that Oria proposed to suffer, for anything but her own self-advancement. "I ask only that we get this over with as quickly as possible. No offense intended to Your Highness."

Full of the lust Lonen so determinedly radiated, though not completely manufactured she felt sure, he tugged on the braid he still held. "A man likes an eager bride."

Though she knew he'd said it to sustain and enlarge on the ruse they perpetuated, the insinuation still made her face go hot. Febe actually leaked some vestiges of sympathy through her *hwil*. It was to her credit that she could at least feel pity for what she imagined Oria would endure. Hopefully Rhianna would never have occasion to tell Febe of the agreement she and Lonen had made. Oria regretted telling her, especially as it had made no difference and potentially exposed them to trouble.

"You'll have to leave that outside, however." High Priestess Febe pointed at Lonen's axe with a gesture very like the Destrye one against magic. Oria had never noticed that similarity before.

"Not a chance, lady," he growled.

"It's an offense against the source of magic."

"Which is why it doesn't leave my body. I've had enough of Báran magic."

"Fine then. But you'll have to remove it for the ceremony itself."

"As long as I have it close to hand," he told her, his posture and energy showing how willingly he'd use it against her if she tried anything to harm him or Oria.

"Enter the temple, then," she intoned, "and we will join you as the moons intended."

Lonen didn't move, though he released Oria's braid. "Just like that? There are no ceremonial preparations?"

"Such as?" High Priestess Febe had already turned to go in, Oria ready to follow on her heels before anyone saw through to the flaws in their story.

"Shouldn't Oria—the princess, that is—have a special gown? Attendants or some such?"

Febe cocked her head at him, puzzlement and suspicion faint on the air. "Come now, Your Highness is good to be solicitous of his captured bride, but this ceremony will simply bind her to you under our laws. I understood you to be in something of a demanding mood. It will not be a temple-blessed marriage, if that's what you're hoping for." Her voice held sudden suspicion.

Oria willed Lonen to play dumb. As if he'd heard her, he said, "What is that?"

Mollified, the high priestess inclined her head. "Merely a local custom, something idealistic young women pine for. The ceremony I shall conduct will be equally binding."

"Proceed then." Lonen retreated to his curt and lustful conqueror role, following in Febe's wake, the priests behind them at a decorous distance, the City Guard remaining outside.

"He is a smart man. Pays attention," Chuffta mused.

"Why is the Destrye king suddenly your new best friend?" It annoyed her more than it should. She'd never had to share Chuffta's affections with anyone.

"I still love you best," he soothed her, *"but he is also concerned about you taking on the Trom and wants to protect you. I like him for that."*

"Then the two of you can sit around and console each other when I do the summoning."

Chuffta tsked at her. *"Such temper."*

"This isn't exactly the best day of my life," she snapped at her Familiar—and then felt bad about it. Just as she had when she'd used Lonen's buried pain to punish him. She'd thought she'd been handling all the changes and challenges so well, but then she combusted into a ball of emotion. Having to ruthlessly suppress any hint of grien—and maintain the façade of *hwil*—around the temple priests and priestesses strained her fragile control even more. Still she didn't need to be full of self-pity. This path had been her idea. She started to apologize to Chuffta, then remembered Lonen's chiding about how she apologized too often, and stopped herself.

But that left her at a loss. How was she supposed to never apologize for anything?

"Maybe by not doing anything worth apologizing for in the first place." It could have sounded huffy, but Chuffta said it like a peace offering, his tail a comforting bracelet around her wrist.

They entered one of the smaller temple ritual spaces, simple and sacrosanct, even though it might not be as grand as the main sanctuary where she would have celebrated her temple-blessed marriage, had it not been for Lonen.

Of course, before the Destrye came, she'd been nowhere near attaining her mask, so a temple-blessed ceremony had remained a distant ambition. Important to keep that firmly in mind.

Febe positioned the two of them before the altar, waited for Lonen to unstrap his axe from his back, instructed them to kneel, then retreated behind the altar. Lonen looked about, then laid the axe by his left hand. To Oria's surprised pleasure, Febe did not banish Chuffta. The temple honored the derkesthai in general, though their relationship to the temple hierarchy tended to be more like Grienon's rapid passage through the skies, his phases ever shifting, now brightly present, then abruptly gone. To Oria, her Familiar was like Sgatha, ever present, looming large in her mind.

Much as Lonen did, occupying her senses and attention. It would be welcome when he finally departed, giving her some peace of mind again. Mental quiet had never been her forte, but the man had a knack for agitating her.

As the High Priestess assembled her tools, saying prayers over the various unguents, consecrating the wine to Sgatha, the grains to Grienon, Lonen spoke to Oria under his breath.

"How does this go?"

"I don't know." She kept her reply barely audible, but the Destrye warrior was not so easily put off.

"How can you not know?"

"I've never seen the ceremony. It's always private. Now, shh."

He didn't like that answer, his energy restive and seeking. "You could have warned me," he had to mutter, which unfortunately made her want to laugh. Exercising firm resolve, she managed not to, but the mask was what saved her from exposing the amusement so not appropriate to a nobly resigned captive bride.

"Maybe not the worst day of your life either," Chuffta noted in the idle tone he liked to use to tease her.

"You hush, too."

"Take a moment to meditate," High Priestess Febe intoned. "Clear your minds. Settle your emotions. Seek *hwil* in your hearts and contemplate the step you take today, with Sgatha and Grienon as your witnesses."

Oria folded her hands together and bowed her head, stilling her sgath so it pooled peacefully, creating the appearance of deep meditation.

"Would you like me to lead you into a true meditative trance?"

"Not now, thank you. I'd rather have my wits about me."

"Done correctly, meditation should result in greater alertness through a relaxed and open mind."

"Yes, well, we've established that I'm terrible at meditating. Leave me alone. It's my wedding day."

Chuffta snorted at that, but let it go.

"What are we supposed to be doing?" Lonen whispered, though High Priestess Febe had left the room.

"Meditating," she hissed back.

"Yes, I heard that part. What in Arill does that mean?"

"Like… praying to your goddess. *Silently,*" she emphasized.

He was quiet for a few breaths, no more. "Now what?"

She tried to suppress the laugh, but failed so it choked out in a most unladylike sound. Lonen flashed a grin at her and she shook her head. "Keep doing it. And be quiet—she could come back at any time."

"Why would I keep doing something I already did?"

"You're supposed to be contemplating!" She tried to sound stern, but his complaints so closely echoed hers through the years that she couldn't manage it.

"Contemplate what?" he groused. "I already made the decision about the step I'm about to take. There's no sense revisiting it."

"Then pretend. It won't be that much longer."

He stayed quiet for a bit more, though he shifted restlessly, looking around the room and studying the various representations of the moons, looking at her from time to time. That insatiable curiosity of his built, feeding into her sgath, slowly intensifying. She was so keenly aware of him, she knew he'd speak the moment before he did.

"You don't mind?" he asked.

"You talking when we're supposed to be meditating?"

"Do you always do what the temple tells you to do?"

"Hardly ever," she admitted. "But appearances are critical. Especially now."

He sighed and was quiet for a while. But his question remained between them, tugging at her like Chuffta pulling her braids when he wanted attention. And it might be some time before Febe returned. She reached out with her sgath to keep tabs on the high priestess, who was indeed still in one of the inner sanctums, no doubt also meditating and preparing herself for the ritual.

"We have a little time and I'll give us warning," she relented. "Do I mind what?"

"Not having a special dress, a big celebration. I don't have a *beah* for you."

"What is a *beah*?"

"A Destrye gifts his bride with a *beah* and she wears it as a symbol of their marriage. I thought I'd have time to find something to stand in place of it until I can give you a proper one. And that we'd have time to change clothes."

"You look fine—I told you before."

"I look like a Báran," he grumped, then glared, annoyance sparking when she giggled. "It's not funny."

"Báran clothes look good on you," she soothed, much as she would Chuffta's offended dignity. Perhaps males of all species were the same.

"Hey!"

She ignored Chuffta's indignant response. Lonen did look appealing in the silk pants and short-sleeved shirt, even though her sgath mainly showed her his exuberant masculine presence.

"Well, you deserve something better than that robe," he

replied. "And more than this hasty ceremony. Arill knows, Natly went on enough about the details of planning..." He trailed off, chagrin coloring his thoughts.

"Yeah," she drawled. "Maybe better to not bring up your fiancée during our actual wedding ceremony."

"Former fiancée," he corrected. "Really not even that. And this isn't the ceremony yet—this is waiting around for it to start. My knees are getting sore."

"And here I thought you were the big, bad warrior."

"I am. Big, bad warriors don't kneel. We charge about, swinging our weapons."

She laughed, shaking her head at him. That good humor of his flickered bright, charming her, banishing his perpetual anger to the shadowed corners of his aura. In the back of her mind, Febe moved. "She's coming back. Not much longer. Try to school your thoughts."

He muttered some Destrye curse at that, but subsided. Oria did her best to still her thoughts. It would be comforting to know ahead what the ceremony entailed, but the temple liked their surprises. The mystery was part of all rituals— intended to catch a person in honest reactions, particularly those that revealed a failure of *hwil*. Something, she now understood, to prevent the inevitable gaming of the system. Whatever the magical binding of the marriage ceremony, it would likely be uncomfortable, perhaps even painful for her. With any luck, Lonen's insensitivity to magic should prevent him from suffering from it.

High Priestess Febe entered the small chapel, bringing such a powerful charge of sgath with her that Oria's illicit grien leaped to devour it, forcing her to choke it back. The High Priestess had been drawing heavily on Bára's magic, using her female sgath to store it up. Priest Vico followed her, taking his place beside her at the altar, his male grien soaking up the sgath and activating the magic. They did not have an ideal partnership, but long practice and Febe's powerful sgath allowed him to perform feats usually reserved for priests of much higher rank. Fortunate, as all of those highly ranked priests had died when the Destrye attacked.

"Princess Oria, you come to the temple to beseech the moons to give you a husband. Is this so?"

"I do." Oria spoke the words firmly. Magic responded to intention and she would start this marriage with a firm one.

"King Lonen has proposed himself to be your husband, to channel your sgath to grien, to be both your walls and your guide to the world. Is he an acceptable choice?"

Ironic, all the truths and untruths in the ritual words. "He is."

"You come as a priestess to the temple and will leave as wife to King Lonen. Remove your mask so you come before him barefaced, and so that he may gaze on the face of his beloved, forevermore known only to him."

She should have expected that, but hadn't. Priest Vico came around behind her with a bowl, a platter for her mask, and bearing the small silver knives the masked used at meal times to cut the ribbons. He set the platter to her left and Oria covered her mask with her palms to hold it in place. Priest Vico cut the ribbons at her temples, sliding them from the knots in her braids. She lowered the mask to the platter, not looking at Lonen, feeling terribly shy though he'd seen her face before she gained her mask. Even so. Quickly she took the cool, scented cloth from the bowl and wiped her face with it, deeply understanding the need for this part of the ritual. It gave her time to compose her expression—and hopefully not look too sweaty or red-faced.

Lonen's comments about her having a pretty gown or time to make herself beautiful as Natly would have done niggled at her. But he wasn't marrying her for her appearance, or out of affection. Better for him to see her truly, without anything prettified between them. *Come before him barefaced.* It took more courage than she'd have thought, but she lowered the cloth to the bowl, and raised her eyes to meet his.

He smiled at her—not that cheeky grin full of mischief, but a more solemn one, gaze roving over her face. A vivid image of him caressing her cheek, then kissing her lips, came from him, and she blushed.

She waited. Knowing the temple, the next phase would likely test her sorely.

"King Lonen," High Priestess Febe intoned, her voice echoing with ripples of sgath, even as Priest Vico's grien seized Oria in a fierce mental grip, "take your bride's hand."

Oria braced herself. Oh, this would be bad indeed.

~ 8 ~

L ONEN HESITATED, STARTLED out of his joy at seeing Oria's face again—so much more exotically beautiful even than he'd remembered, her eyes an even brighter coppery brown than in his dreams—taken aback by the strange request.

Much as he'd been hoping to find a way around the restriction against touching Oria's skin, he believed her that it would be painful for her, even damaging. And surely her temple brethren knew this. The twin masks of the priest and priestess behind the ornate altar both seemed to frown at him. These Bárans couldn't do anything simply. Everything had to be tied up in magical ritual and other assorted nastiness. Oria should be able to put on a pretty dress, accept his *beah* before Arill, and then dance the night away in his arms. Before spending the rest of it in his bed.

Not … whatever it was that loomed ahead of them, putting his short hairs on end.

Oria solved his dilemma by taking his hand, lacing her slim fingers between his in a grip as fierce as her bones were delicate. A small sound escaped her, she swayed, and Chuffta coiled more of his tail around her other wrist, even wrapping his sinuous neck around hers.

"Get on with it," Lonen growled at Febe, grateful his role as rampaging conqueror allowed him to force things along.

The priestess didn't like it, her posture full of disapproval, but she similarly joined hands with the priest who'd returned to her side after cutting away Oria's mask, and he raised his other hand in a gesture Lonen knew well. From the battle mages it had meant a fireball or earthquake soon to come, and he had to throttle back his now-instinctive reach for his axe.

Instead something strong, yet not entirely painful, grabbed him, darkening his vision until he seemed to be in another place. Almost like a dream, one of those surreal ones when Oria had visited his nights, prowling through his mind and consuming him body and soul. She was there in this place, too, holding his hand and—not exactly smiling at him—but looking deeply into his eyes, her copper gaze bright and sparking like candle flames. Lines of pain bracketed her pretty mouth and he tried to let go of her. She held on as tenaciously as in any of his dreams, when he'd been unable to muster the will to stop her from milking his cock or devouring his heart.

He was marrying this woman. A woman of foreign ideas and powerful magic. They'd be bound together for the rest of their lives. The yawning chasm of that future opened beneath his feet, black with terrifying and exhilarating possibilities.

Febe and the mysterious priest appeared in the dream also, golden masks glowing with otherworldly light, their crimson robes dark as old blood. Chuffta seemed to hover nearby, a blaze of white.

The priest held a shining blade in his hand, a knife made of glass that radiated a light as brightly silver blue as Grienon at full face. Oria turned their joined hands so her wrist faced up and his down. The blade struck, slicing first her fair skin where the blood showed in a delicate blue tracery, then his browner flesh from beneath, a breathtakingly bright pang. She never flinched—perhaps because she could no more move than he could—but her copper eyes darkened, the lines around her mouth deepening with the sharp pain.

It burned him, both her suffering and the hot flow of blood from his wrist. The priest handed the glass blade to the priestess, and reached out, placing a palm over each of their wounds. Oria screamed, a thin and weak sound, and Lonen tried to reach for her, still unable to move. Then the burn overtook him too, climbing up his arm until it struck his heart like a tree viper's poison. His turn to shout the agony of it, his heart racing nearly to burst.

But he couldn't break from Oria's gaze, her ever-darkening eyes filling his vision, her blood arcing into his, then flowing back, her heart pounding in staccato beats, humming like the jewelbirds she'd spoken of.

They'd become so black, her eyes, that they lost every glint of copper, going flat and dull, densely matte. With a chord of terror, he recognized those eyes, that life-sucking gaze. Identical to the Trom that had killed his father and brother.

The scene from the council chambers roared back at him, a crystal clear memory—Oria confronting the thing even as Lonen fought Arnon's restraining grip, trying against all reason to save her, his enemy, from that lethal touch that turned men to boneless pulp. The Trom had caressed her cheek, spoken to her in some tangled tongue. And nothing happened to her.

She alone had survived the monster's instantly delivered death.

Now the thing's eyes looked back out of her and once again he couldn't move to reach her. He fought the suffocating clutch of magic. Though he should be terrified of her, his heart didn't understand that. He fought, not to release her hand, but to bring her closer.

"Oria!"

Her name echoed without sound inside his skull.

And abruptly they were back in that temple room, his knees aching from the stone steps. Oria grasped his hand, fingers still interlaced with his, eyes once again lustrous copper, stared into his, wide with shock.

"Your bride is yours to do with as you wish." The voices of the priest and priestess came as if from another realm. There they stood, once again behind the altar—or had they ever truly moved?—speaking the words in unison, some aspect of the magic giving them a strange harmonic. "Her magic is yours to use, her body yours from which to draw succor and heirs."

They had to be ritual words because they knew perfectly well Lonen had no ability to access magic. But it confirmed what the Destrye had suspected, long ago on that battlefield when they'd decided to kill the masked sorcerers on the walls, in hopes of stopping the flow of magic to the battle mages. *Her magic is yours to use.* Though he couldn't use it as a Báran man would, guilt plucked at him, as he intended to use her just as ruthlessly. To save his people, yes, but he'd treat her as a tool as surely as any of these sorcerers would have. Just in different way. *Yours to use.*

Oria's hand trembled in his, her eyes blank, her face pale. Something nudged at Lonen's fingers and he started, glancing down to find the pointed tip of Chuffta's tail wedging gently between their joined hands. Mortified, he yanked them apart. Like a child's doll suddenly discarded, Oria crumpled to the stone floor. Lonen barely caught her in time, carefully touching her only over the silk, even though one of Chuffta's wings abruptly spread for balance buffeted his face.

He sat back, adjusting her so her head pillowed on his thigh, wanting more than anything to smooth back the damp tendrils of coppery hair plastered to her temples, her skin so waxy translucent that the shadowy foramina of her skull showed through. It seemed a terrible omen, this death's head, so like all the decomposed dead he'd seen over the last years.

Chuffta crawled gently onto her bosom, using the thumb claws at the bend of his wings to steady his progress. He'd done that before, when Oria lost consciousness outside the gates of the city. Hopefully he'd help her recover this time as well.

"What's wrong with her?" Lonen hardened his voice, so as to sound demanding, rather than pleading. Although he could likely drop the charade. They were married and that couldn't be reversed. The Báran ritual might be cruel, but it did seem to work on a deeper level than a Destrye marriage. Or so he assumed. None had mentioned anything like this following Arill's ceremony. The permanence of the bond resonated even in his mind-dead skull. Oria lurked in there, a part of him now. Odd, but also reassuring to sense her life force when she looked so very close to death.

"The Princess Oria is fragile." The High Priestess assumed a tone of apology, though she seemed nearly gleeful. "Perhaps we should have warned you better, King of the Destrye—your prize may not be long lived. Best to enjoy her while you can."

"Better to read your own histories, Your Highness," the priest advised, sounding more somber. "The Báran women taken by your kind are like tropical flowers consigned to eternal winter. Princess Oria will never bloom in your harsh land. Take your pleasure of her if you must. We cannot stop you from claiming your right. If she survives the night, however ... I ask Your Highness to consider that it would be a kindness to leave her here." He paid no attention to Febe's intake of breath, though she otherwise showed little sign of her disapproval. "You have no cause to love Bára, King Lonen," he continued, "and much reason, perhaps to hate us and Princess Oria along with our people. But she has done you and the Destrye no wrong."

"I know that," Lonen replied, speaking only to the priest. "You are a good and loyal subject to speak for her at this time. I'll remember you to her."

High Priestess Febe remained where she was, but the priest came around to hold a hand over Oria, murmuring something that sounded like a prayer. Chuffta didn't bridle at the man, so Lonen trusted he only helped, not harmed. Indeed, Oria's face, while it didn't exactly regain color, at least looked a bit more like she belonged to the land of the living and not as if her spirit lingered in whatever witchy realm they'd traveled to for the wedding ritual.

"Take her to her tower," the priest murmured. "Priestess Juli will be there as her attendant and will know what to do for her." With a last wiggle of his fingers, he nodded to Lonen and left.

Taking the advice to heart, Lonen strapped his axe onto his back, careful not to jostle Oria unnecessarily, then gathered his unconscious wife into his arms, keeping the silk robes between his hands and her slight body. Chuffta took wing to make it easier for him. As the time before, it struck him how little she weighed, like a jewelbird herself, all brilliantly colored feathers over hollow bones.

"We need to stop doing this," he muttered at her, rising to his feet. He braced himself for Chuffta's piercing talons as the derkesthai landed on his shoulder, prehensile tail snaking out to coil gently around Oria's throat, the slim white column exposed by her laxly tipped back head. He'd have to get padded shoulders for his garments, too, as it seemed the Familiar would become a fixture in his life.

High Priestess Febe stood before him, golden mask re-mote. "Take your bride and go." She set Oria's mask, still on the little tile they'd put it on, onto Oria's breast.

"I intend to." Though if Febe assumed he'd leave Bára immediately, she'd be in for a surprise. One he'd enjoy. Forcing her to call Oria queen would be a well-earned triumph. "Shouldn't you tie the mask on her again, if I'm the only one to see her face forever more?"

The priestess checked a small movement, then inclined her head. "Those words are a formality, not meant to apply to other close family or temple ceremonies, but as you say, Your Highness." She retrieved a covered box, opening the colorful lid to show a spool of golden ribbons within. With deft, practiced movements, she cut away the threads of the ribbons still attached to Oria's mask at three points—the temple, cheek and jaw—then attached new ones, moving behind and around Oria, weaving the ribbons into her braids.

"It seems like it would be easier to simply untie them than to cut them every time and have to fetch new ones," he commented, as the process took some time.

"You understand nothing of magic, Destrye," the High Priestess replied in an absorbed tone, without rancor, but something of that otherworldly hum to it. "Which may well be your future undoing. You trifle with powers beyond your reckoning. If you want my advice, take your prize and go back to Dru. Against all odds you have achieved a short victory over your betters. Savor that, yes, in the tradition of your ancestors, but do not linger. Bára will only bring you grief. In your land you might have something of a pleasurable life as King of the Destrye. But you will never be King of Bára."

"Am I to believe that's some sort of magical prophecy?" He allowed a sneer, and for his deep dislike of this woman to rise up. Hopefully she'd detect it in him as Oria would.

Finished, the High Priestess stepped back and laced her fingers together over her belly. "You would be wise to recognize it as such, Your Highness, but from what I've witnessed, wisdom is not a virtue Grienon bestowed upon you."

Perhaps not. Nolan had been universally acknowledged as the most intelligent of King Archimago's sons, and he'd died first. Ion had been the most courageous, the heir and all that the Destrye could wish for in their next king, and he'd died too, gone in an instant. Lonen might never make a wise or noble king, but he was what the Destrye had. Arnon would serve, in the event of Lonen's demise, but his younger brother would make an even more reluctant king, far happier with his building plans, designs, and aqueducts.

But, though he might lack wisdom, Lonen knew a snow job when he saw one. The future belonged to those who took it by the throat and made it what they wanted it to be. Oria knew that, too.

"With all respect to your office, High Priestess," he said, allowing a feral grin to bare his teeth, "you can consign your supposed prophecies—and your wretched advice—to the nearest chasm."

Turning his back on the woman, he carried Oria up to her tower.

THE CLIMB, OF course, took forever. Fortunately, during their time in the temple the sun had set and Sgatha risen, shedding her soft rose light. Which meant they'd been in there for hours. Another reason to dislike magic—it distorted the senses. But the night breezes cooled the air, blowing in the open arched windows that riddled Oria's tower, making it look more like lacework than stone from below. Chuffta had thankfully resumed his station on Oria's breast, watching her face with devotion worthy of any hunting hound.

By the time he reached the summit of the endlessly spiraling stairs, Lonen gave thanks that he'd ignored Natly's protestations that manual labor was beneath the dignity of a king. All those trenches dug, beams lifted, and sacks of seed hauled given him the endurance for the climb. Even Oria's slight body felt like the heaviest bag of grain, his legs wobbly with effort when he finally reached the top stair.

He stood there stupidly a moment—his brain almost unable to grasp that the unending ascent had, in fact, ended—uncertain of his next move. The ceremony had perhaps taxed him far more than he had felt at the time. He almost envied Oria her deep sleep.

"King Lonen." A crimson-robed, golden-masked priestess appeared before him as if by magic. "Bring her in here. What happened to the princess?"

He followed her, impossibly weary, through the high-ceilinged hall that lead to Oria's rooftop garden. Instead of going straight through, however, the priestess turned into a branching corridor, opening a set of doors into an airy chamber, bright and ethereal as Oria herself. The woman drew gauzy curtains aside from a bed unlike any he'd seen. He lowered Oria onto it, feeling absurdly like some hero out of a tale.

Only in those the hero rescued the princess, rather than being the cause of her injuries.

"Are you Juli?"

"Yes, Your Highness." She curtseyed to him with grave ceremony. Something, however, about the red curls escaping her braids to form a sprightly halo around her mask made him think she wasn't always so decorous.

"The wedding ceremony," he told her. "It required us to hold hands. Oria suffered from my touch and collapsed immediately after. She hasn't been conscious since. The priest said you would know how to help her."

"Yes, Your Highness. I'll do what I can." She set to gathering supplies, working with deft efficiency. "You are wed then—the binding worked?"

He hadn't been aware there was any question of that. "According to High Priestess Febe, yes. Is there something I should know?"

Juli shrugged, a graceful gesture like a dancer's. "Surely Your Highness understands that Bárans don't wed foreigners. So, no, there was no certainty, even though Princess Oria believed her own magic would be enough to seal the bond, and give her access to the relationship you hold with your people."

"I'm a king crowned on the battlefield. There's nothing magical about that." Feeling worse than useless, he sat in a chair that looked too spindly to hold his weight. It creaked perilously, but held. For the time being.

"All life holds magic," Juli replied, brewing some potion with meticulous measurements. "Only of different potencies. Here in Bára, we've condensed and refined it to our purpose. In Dru, you have trees as tall as our towers, isn't it true, Your Highness?"

"Some of them nearly so, yes."

"And yet they come from a seed I could fit in the palm of

my hand. How is that not magical? Here now, Master Chuffta, scoot a bit so I can reach her." The Familiar obliged with a rustle of wings and Juli used a small silver knife to cut the ribbons on Oria's mask. With an attitude of reverence, she set the molded gold thing on a tile next to the bed, clearly kept there for exactly that purpose. Strange people, the Bárans, with their masks and wasteful practices.

He watched Juli tip the fluid between Oria's lips, feeding it to her in delicate sips, all the while careful not to touch her. "Your touch harms her also?"

Juli nodded, the curls springing like coiled lamplight. "Not as much as yours, Your Highness—no insult intended—because I am first Báran and second highly trained in *hwil*, which is why I was chosen to attend her. But she's been pushed past her breaking point, so I won't add to the strain."

"What is *hwil*?" Might as well seek to extend his knowledge while he sat about being useless to his wife. And possibly to the Destrye. If Oria didn't recover, all of this would be for naught. He didn't know what he could do then, except perhaps to go home and at least die with them.

Not a pleasant option.

"It's a core teaching of our temple," Juli was explaining. "It means achieving a peaceful state of mind that allows us to contain our emotional energies. My excellent *hwil* makes me a restful person for her to be around."

Which meant, by reverse logic, that he himself would not be restful to Oria. He had zero idea how one went about containing their emotional energy. Or how to know what it was in the first place. He spread his hands, looking at them for any indication of what came out of his skin that affected Oria so. On his right wrist, a livid scar pulsed an angry red—and yet far more healed than it ought to be already. He knew how to wield his battle axe, how to lead his warriors, maybe something of the endless cascade of decision-making that made up being king, even something of farming and building aqueducts, now, but he didn't know how to keep from harming his own wife with those hands.

"Will she be all right?" He sounded plaintive and for once he didn't care. Exhaustion had him by the balls and he suddenly felt he couldn't rise from that chair, much less help Oria or anyone else. Never had he felt his own mortality so keenly.

"I believe so, Your Highness. She recovered from a far graver condition before, and she's much stronger now in her magic than she was then."

"The other time I touched her."

"Well, yes and no, Your Highness—many stresses conspired to cause Princess Oria's collapse at the surrender of Bára." She said it as if it were part of a legend. Probably it was. Wonderful. He'd go down in Báran history as the worst of fiends. Not that he didn't deserve it.

"You might as well call me Lonen. As your mistress's attendant, you'll likely be in my company a great deal. The Destrye don't much stand on ceremony."

"Then you plan to stay in Bára? The rumor mill had you riding off with the princess before Grienon rose."

He snorted at that. One thing the Bárans and Destrye shared—a love of gossip, particularly about the royal families. "We're here to stay for the time being." He stopped there, unsure of how much of Oria's ambitions she'd shared with her waiting woman. "You're not much like the others," he noted.

"No, Your Highness? How not?"

"Oria is forever telling me the answers to my questions are temple secrets. She confides very little." He waited to see if Juli would reveal how much Oria had confided in her.

Juli straightened, rubbing her palms briskly on her robes, as if drying them, or shedding dirt. "May I speak frankly, Your Highness?"

"Lonen. And please do. I've had a surfeit of secrets and Báran double-talk." He rubbed a hand over his brow, his eyelids heavy. Oria seemed to be resting a more natural sleep, however, and even Chuffta dozed, green eyes slitted as he crouched beside her on the fancy of a bed.

"Forgive me, Your—Lonen." Juli began mixing several new potions, measuring them into various containers, then combining them into a single goblet. "I should have realized the wedding ceremony would exhaust you also. This will be restorative and also let you sleep."

She handed him the pretty Báran glass and he studied it dubiously. Ion would have knocked it from his hand, lest the foreign sorceress seek to poison him. Or kill him in his sleep. "I should stay awake. Keep watch."

Juli put her hands on her hips, conveying an affectionate exasperation that reminded him of his mother, though the priestess couldn't be much older than himself. "You rode straight here from Dru, yes? Probably sleeping little on the journey and starting well before dawn today."

When he grudgingly nodded, she pointed at the glass he still held. "The temple ceremonies drain even the most stalwart, those in the best of health. There will be no staying awake for you. The tower is well protected. I'm sure you noted the guards below as you entered."

He had, bemused by their crisp, deferential salutes, instead of challenges, and total lack of surprise that he carried their unconscious princess.

"And Master Chuffta himself is no minor obstacle. Rest is

what you and Oria both need."

"Not until you tell me whatever frank words you sought permission to say."

She faced him, cocking her head. "She has to be careful of you, Lonen. I say this as her friend as well as her serving woman and priestess attendant. Oria has not been much among people outside her family and priestesses like myself, all of whom have served her with perfect *hwil*. She is powerful, yes, but that power comes with a price that requires a delicate balance. Wedding you is an extraordinary step for her to take. One might say it's a choice so courageous as to be foolhardy. You could easily kill her—or worse. There you sit, hesitating to drink a healing potion from me because you fear poison. Surely you must see that you seem no less dangerous to us."

She had a point. And, he supposed, he'd already made a choice—one Ion would have beaten him bloody for considering—in marrying Oria and living among the Bárans at least as long as it took her to access those secrets she needed.

Lonen drained the glass, grimacing at the bitter flavor, handed it back to Juli, and wrapped one fist in his other hand, feeling the pull of the new wound. "Am I so terrible?"

"You are..." She hesitated.

Big, came Oria's voice in his head. *And you carry a great big battle-axe.*

"Formidable," Juli decided, and he thought she smiled behind her mask. "You radiate emotional energy as fierce as the sun's heat in summer."

"I don't know how stop doing that." He set his jaw in frustration, though it bled quickly away into lassitude. Juli's potion worked fast.

"Let me help you, Your Highness." Juli knelt at his feet, removing his slippers, then helped him sit up in the chair, nimble fingers finding the buckles of the shoulder harness, freeing him of it. She wedged a shoulder under his and levered him to his feet, though he tried to resist.

"My touch won't hurt you?" His words came out slightly slurred.

"Some." Her voice held strain, though that could be from his weight. She possessed a surprising amount of strength, her frame far sturdier than Oria's, walking him around to the far side of the bed, between Oria and the doors. "But my *hwil* protects me and I have nothing like Oria's sensitivity. It is both her blessing and her curse."

"Seems like mostly a curse to me."

"Only because she has yet to fully grow into her abilities—and you've seen very little as yet that she's already capable of. She will be a sorceress beyond compare, and a queen to go down in legend."

So, Oria had shared her plans. That was good. Though he couldn't recall why. Befuddled, he sat on the side of the bed and Juli undid the ties at his throat, then pulled the shirt over his head. "I'm sleeping here?"

"Yes." She eased him back on the pillows, the silk cool against his hot skin. A breeze scented with Oria's lilies wafted from the terrace. His eyes closed of their own accord. "Keep the sheet between you, but it's good for you to be with her. You're Oria's husband now. We're counting on you to take good care of her."

She draped another silk sheet over him, again reminding him of his mother, and days of boyhood long gone, when he'd slept without fear of dreaming. He might be dreaming already, Juli's voice a musical whisper like the moonlit breeze.

"Sgatha knows, no one else will."

~ 9 ~

S HE FLOATED THROUGH gray mists, remembering them from before. Which helped her not fight them. Instead, she accepted the way the mists wrapped her in cocoons of enshrining silk that healed her, as if she were a butterfly, soon to emerge with damp wings and no more duties than kissing flowers. That might be lovely—a life of nothing but the sugar offered by flowers and the sun on her colorful self, bringing a sigh of joy to someone's lips.

"Until a bird snapped you up."

She knew that wry mind-voice, too. Chuffta, her Familiar. Memories came back faster this time, too—good. Cracking open dry eyelids, she squinted at his triangular face, the large eyes green as new leaves in spring, his white scales shining iridescent in the rising sunlight.

"Welcome back to the land of the living," he said.

She tried to think back, recover more from the blank mists. "Did I break again?"

"Well, really you just chipped a little. Juli patched you up so the cracks don't even show and you only slept a good long night rather than days."

"What happened? Did the—"

A jagged snore interrupted her and she flipped her head on the pillow to take in the darkly haired and burly Destrye on the other side of the bed. Lonen. Her—

"Husband. Congratulations on your felicitous union. Worst wedding night in history, however."

"Oh hush."

It was good to see him again with her physical eyes. Lonen lay on his back, face relaxed so the scar that cut from his forehead, over one eye and down his cheek didn't pull to the side as it did when he was awake. More scars criss-crossed his chest and concave belly—funny that her sgath didn't show them. She tried looking with both sights at the same time, something she hadn't quite mastered the trick of. The overlapping images tended to make her dizzy. No one else admitted to it, but she nursed a theory that the temple had developed the custom of the masks exactly because they helped prevent that sort of double-vision.

Relinquishing sgath sight again was far more restful. Besides, she liked seeing Lonen with her actual eyes. Her husband. The bond resonated in the deepest part of her. Unreal.

His black hair curled in wild disarray, a dark contrast to the pale silk of the pillows. Dressed only in light trousers, and with one arm flung over his head, his body looked long and powerful—and his manhood tented those trousers dramatically, making her yank her gaze away again.

Something else to put on the list of intimidating things about him.

Just then he drew in another rumbling snore, which cut off in a mutter of blurred words, and she rolled her eyes at Chuffta. *"I slept through that?"*

"He didn't do it all night. He's been making more sounds and thrashing around just in the last little while. Dreaming, maybe? It seemed to be what woke you up."

As if to verify the words, Lonen kicked at something, then shouted. "Go on! Get out of here!" The hand flung over his head clenched into a fist, his muscles flickering, though the arm barely moved. He shouted again, anger and fear coiling around him, his words unclear, as if he spoke through deep water. Then he growled, more like a beast than a man. His eyes rocketed under his lids and he made a strangled cry.

Not knowing what to do, Oria sat up and reached out a tentative hand. She'd touched his hair before—and he hers—without any effect, but she could hardly tug on that to wake him. It seemed far too callous.

"What should I do?"

"I wouldn't want to be having that dream, whatever it is."

Okay then. "Lonen," she called softly—and with no result. He tossed his head on the pillow, crying out broken, inarticulate sounds, that pierced her heart. Jagged images of blood, death, and pain danced through the turmoil of emotions. Those dark things didn't belong in the dancing light of morning. "Lonen…" she tried louder. To no avail. Could he even hear her?

"Lonen!" she nearly shouted, layering in imperious command. "Wake up!"

His eyes flew open, seeing the dream still, one hand snapping to his side, before he went entirely still, the hard granite of his gaze taking in the ceiling, then landing on her, and softening while a smile spread across his face. "Oria." He breathed her name like a meditative chant. "You're better."

His gaze dropped to her breasts, making her realize she wore nothing but her very thin chemise. Juli must have taken off her priestess robes and loosened the ties of the undergarment, because the neckline gaped open, showing a substantial amount of skin. Self-conscious, she drew the cloth together and pushed her hair back from her forehead, snagging it in the tangled braids. She'd slept in them, which would make them an unholy mess to desnarl.

The least of her problems, really.

Giving it up, she drew up the sheet higher, using the movement to scoot back a little from his rapidly intensifying sexual energy. "You were dreaming."

He grimaced, then sat up, too, and scrubbed his hands over his scalp. The curls sprang back in the same bountiful disarray as before, but he didn't seem to notice. "Yeah. I do sometimes. Sorry if I disturbed you."

"More like you disturbed yourself." She wasn't sure if a hard man like him would welcome comfort. "It sounded bad."

"Sometimes they are." He shrugged it off, chagrin and irritation both rippling off him with the gesture. "Made Natly crazy. Said she couldn't sleep with me fighting golems all night. Yelling and kicking and such like."

Ah, so she'd shared his bed. Though, of course Oria had known that—had glimpsed their lovemaking in Lonen's head, much as she hadn't wanted to. Of course they'd slept together afterwards.

"So she stopped—sleeping with me, I mean." Lonen watched her with gray eyes gone clear and calm, now that the dregs of the nightmare had left him. "And I didn't much care, I found."

Curious. "Why not?"

"Because a lot of those dreams weren't fighting golems, but were having sex with you." He grinned. "It kind felt disloyal to be longing for you *and* keeping her from a good night's sleep while doing it. Ah, there it is. I like being able to see you blush again."

She clapped hands over her cheeks, which did feel hot. "I

should put on my mask."

He stopped her as she reached for it, carefully catching the trailing cuff of her undergarment. "Don't. Not yet. During the… ceremony, or whatever in Arill you'd call that thing we endured, Febe said I alone get to see your face, something about a husband's privilege."

Of course that would be customary. Her own parents had always removed their masks once private with each other, and with their children. She hadn't thought of that aspect. She and Lonen would not have children to share her face with, but she would have him. She drew her hand back, leaving the mask where it sat, though she felt exceptionally exposed.

The wedding ritual had been something to endure, for sure, and she wouldn't blame him for being unsettled, even frightened by it. Much as in her own testing, something in the binding light had looked out at her. Like the Trom and yet not. It spoke to her without words, though she imagined the hissing voice. *Princess Ponen.* She shuddered at the memory and Lonen tipped his head, studying her. "Cold?"

As if. The morning heat already sat heavy on the day, not a breeze stirring. "We should get up."

"Should we?"

"I should summon Juli. We'll need to eat."

"We have time for that. The council meeting isn't until this afternoon, right? And Juli said you were to rest."

Well, yes. But it felt… dangerous to be in bed with him, with his masculine exuberance sizzling hot on her skin and his gaze wandering over her, seeing more than anyone ever had. She wasn't at all sure how to handle him, what one did with a husband in one's bed in the morning. When one couldn't do the normal thing. Even then. "Do you want to tell me about your nightmare then?"

He gave her a curious look. "I figured you would have seen it in my head."

"No. Just fragments and … feelings." She fidgeted with the sheet. "I really do try not to prowl about in your mind. It's more that you sometimes project images rather forcefully—as you know, since you've discovered how to do it deliberately."

He grinned, unrepentant. "Seems only fair, to balance out the power. But I don't project the same way when I'm asleep and dreaming?"

"Perhaps it's the nature of dreams—nothing coherent came through."

"I have some privacy there then."

"Yes." She twisted the sheet in her fingers, choking back the apology that wanted to spill out.

"I was fighting the Trom," he offered. "They were at the door, trying to get in and I was afraid they'd get to you. And then I turned, and you were one of them, coming at me with your hand upraised, and I knew you'd kill me."

By Sgatha's light, it wouldn't be so. "It was only a dream," she managed to say around a tongue gone thick and dry.

"I know that. And still it seemed—I don't know. During that ritual I thought I saw something odd about your eyes."

"I barely remember anything about that ritual." She laughed, but it came out far too ragged and breathless.

It worked well enough to distract him, though, because he smiled with her. "That was a hell of a thing, wasn't it? You'll like our wedding in Arill's temple much better. It will actually be pleasant. Fun even. I have to tell you, Oria—you Bárans do *not* know how to have a good time."

"Yes, well, dealing with the magics that we do, we have to be a disciplined people. The temple and its rituals safeguard us in myriad ways. We observe rules to make sure the magic doesn't destroy us, or that we don't destroy each other."

"Disciplines like *hwil*." He studied her face intently for a reaction and she regretted that her mask sat so far away.

"What do you know about *hwil*?" She sounded, and felt, stiff.

"Juli told me some, last night when I brought you here."

"Juli shouldn't have—"

"Juli realizes that I'm going to need to know some of these things that you think to withhold from me. This is an important aspect of your life—and of any possibility that we'll be able to touch each other—so I think it's obviously valuable for me to be aware of its properties."

"Understanding *hwil* won't change anything, Lonen." She realized she'd clenched her hands into fists by the bite of her nails into her palms. "I can't just *learn* to bear someone else's touch."

"How do you know—have you ever tried?"

"What I've tried is to explain that I haven't had much opportunity to practice any of this!"

"Don't get all huffy with me." He pushed a few pillows into a better position and leaned back against them, stretching lazily and then putting his hands behind his neck, displaying his furred chest to excellent effect. "Tell me what *hwil* feels like."

"How am I supposed to do that?"

"First of all, relax. We're just having a conversation."

"In bed." Practically naked.

His smile stretched across his face as lazily as the rest. "A good place for it. How about this—do you have a hair brush?"

"Why?"

"Your braids are all messed up and it looks uncomfortable. Maybe you'll feel better if I take them down for you."

"You're obsessed with my hair." Though the snarled things

were pulling uncomfortably.

He shrugged a little, gray eyes dancing with that mischief that sparked in blue stars from him. "I can't deny it. Get your hair brush, Oria."

She huffed out an impatient sigh, but got out of bed to retrieve the thing—though taking a moment to tie the neckline of her undergarment closed. The man was as relentless as Chuffta chewing a bone.

"Hey!"

"You know you are. Speaking of, have you hunted recently?"

"Want some alone time with the new mate, huh? I can do that." The derkesthai stretched his wings, yawned mightily, then took off out the open terrace doors.

"Where's Chuffta going?"

"To hunt. Since we'll be here for a while." She stood uncertainly, holding the brush, arrested by Lonen's intent expression and a wave of particularly intense desire from him. "What?"

"With the light behind you like that, your gown is nearly transparent. I can see all the lines of your body."

She grabbed up her gown, wrapping it tight around her.

"Don't do that, Oria," Lonen coaxed. "You're so beautiful. I love seeing you."

A whisper of pleasure ran through her at that. Ah, vanity. "Well—I shouldn't give you ... ideas."'

"I'll tell you a secret." His smile went crooked and he lowered his voice to a loud whisper. "I already have the ideas."

She had no response to that, so she indicated a chair with the brush. "Want me to sit here?"

Lonen spread his legs and patted the sheet covering him between them. "You come here."

"I can't—"

"I won't touch your skin," he said, calm and insistent, but a challenge glittering in his gaze. "Trust me."

"Fine." Aware she'd huffed again, making him laugh at her, she smacked the glass handle of the brush into his palm hard enough to sting, then climbed onto the bed to sit cross-legged between his spread thighs, carefully adjusting the long chemise so it covered her. He waited for her to settle, then began carefully plucking at the braids, unwinding them and undoing the ribbons that held the ends.

"My mask knife is right there," she said, "if you want to cut the ribbons instead."

"Why not just untie them? It's wasteful to be cutting them all the time."

She didn't have a ready reply. "I never thought about it. You think about wastefulness more than I do."

"A Destrye trait, I suppose. We don't have all the riches you do in Bára, so we're careful of what we do have." He had one braid unplaited already, picking up the brush again to smooth it through the loosened locks. "I've never seen hair like yours before. It looks like metal, hammered to a bright polish. I'd like to have your *beah* made of copper just like this, to match, if that's all right with you."

Uncomfortable, she shrugged a little. "It doesn't matter to me."

"It matters to me." His voice stayed even, but annoyance seeped from him.

"Lonen..." She tried to think of a way to explain without making him angry. "I see what you're trying to do here and—"

"What am I trying to do?" he interrupted. Not irritated, but drawing her out with the teasing tone.

She pressed her lips together. She would not amuse him further by huffing. "You know perfectly well."

"Yes, but I want to know what *you* think I'm doing, as I'm not able to read *your* thoughts and emotions." He had more braids undone, and worked at a stubborn one, tugging a little. "Sorry—these are very tangled."

"I'm sure. I don't usually sleep in them. I can call Juli. You don't have to do this."

He kept a hold of the braids when she started to move away. "Oh no, you don't. You're not wriggling out of this so easily. Besides, I'm enjoying myself." He was good at it, too, surprisingly deft.

"I wouldn't think a man like you would want to tend a lady's hair."

"A man like me?"

"You know. Big, strong warrior."

His amusement went sharp, desire heightening. "Not any woman. You. What do you think I'm trying to do?"

"You never give up, do you?"

"No, so you might as well capitulate, my captive bride."

That shouldn't give her a shiver of answering desire. Likely it came of being so close physically, surrounded by his feelings, his usual intense sexuality more sensual, echoing his lazy mood.

"I think you're trying to seduce me," she finally said.

"Of course I am."

"I can't believe you admit it."

"Stop wiggling—I don't want to cut your hair by accident and this ribbon is too knotted to untie. There's no 'admitting' to it. You're my wife, Oria, I want us to be easy together. I want you to trust me."

She sighed for his obstinacy. "It's not a real marriage. Ow!" She clapped a hand to the braid he'd tugged sharply.

"Then don't say untrue things. You were there for that

Arill-cursed ceremony. I might be mind-dead but I can feel the bond to you inside me. We're married as married gets and I'm not spending the rest of my life tied to a woman who dances around me like a deer darting into the shadows at every movement."

She wanted to protest that she didn't do that, but she probably did. "It's not you, though. It's because of how I am."

"You said I intimidate you."

"Badgering me into staying in bed with you and letting you brush my hair while we're both nearly naked is not making me feel less intimidated," she snapped.

He laughed, a low and sensual sound. "Yes it is, because you're all imperious princess again instead of skittish doe. Besides," he leaned close enough that his breath wafted over her ear as he spoke, "we could be a lot more naked than this."

"No, thank you," she replied, making herself stop knotting her chemise, deliberately smoothing it out.

"Nothing to make a person less intimidating than the intimacy of nakedness," he murmured, his voice doing strange things to her.

"There's no point in it," she protested, but she didn't sound nearly firm enough.

"Sure there is. You're a beautiful woman and you're mine. I want to be able to see you in all your loveliness. It will be an enduring delight to me."

"You don't know that."

"Oh, I have a pretty good idea." He nearly purred with sensual confidence and her body seemed to hum along.

He'd gotten all the braids undone and slowly dragged the brush through her hair with one hand, combing the fingers of his other hand through it in alternating strokes. So soothing. How it could feel totally different than when Juli performed this service, she didn't know. But it did. Determined to stay on point, she ignored the melting sensations.

"I understand that you're determined to find a way to have sex with me, but this will only lead to frustration and heartbreak for us both. You saw for yourself what happened from only holding hands with me."

He was quiet a bit, the only sounds the hiss of the hairbrush and the ebullient morning songs of the birds in her garden.

"Juli said it wasn't as bad this time, that you're stronger than you were."

"Obviously not strong enough." The bitterness crept into her voice, curse it. So much self-pity. "Believe me—I don't like being this way." *Worst wedding night ever.*

"Then we find a way to make you stronger."

"Things aren't that easy, Lonen. I can't just wish up being like your copper metal instead of badly blown glass, riddled with flaws. Magic doesn't just make things appear from thin air."

"How does it work?"

"It depends on the kind of magic."

"What kind do you have?"

"My kind." *Princess Ponen.*

"You're avoiding answering my questions."

"Yes. You're not the only stubborn person in this bed."

He burst out laughing, the rush of delight showering around her like a cooling rain. "I'll tell you a story then. When we left Dru to come to Bára and try to end who or what had sent the golems to attack us, I figured I'd never make it home. None of us did. We barreled up all the food and water we had left—which wasn't much—and sent it with everyone who wasn't a warrior on what we called the Trail of New Hope.

Mostly the women and children, but also our scholars, artists, scribes, and a few fighters in case the golems pursued them."

"Where were they going?"

"Somewhere new." She felt the shrug in the rhythm of his hands. "We couldn't stay in Dru any longer, so they went in hopes of finding a place where they could live. My father, brothers, and I took all the warriors to Bára, certain that we'd die trying to fight you. Theirs was a journey of hope and ours of hopelessness in the face of an impossible task. Our main goal was to maybe take enough of you with us to ensure the others could escape."

"I'm sorry," she whispered, daunted by the waves of remembered angry despair coming from him.

"Don't be," he said, sharply. Then the strength of the emotion dimmed. "Is that better?"

"How did you know I was feeling it?"

"You get all tense in your neck and shoulders, and flinch away from me. I'm trying to learn to notice when I'm affecting you and pull it back. Did it work?"

"Yes," she answered, surprised. "Much better."

"See? There are many ways to undo knots. Now, I didn't tell you that story so you'd apologize, yet again, for something you didn't do. I told you so that you'd understand that I already accomplished the impossible. I not only lived, but the Destrye emerged victorious from our hopelessness. My people returned to Dru and we have a fighting chance at surviving the winter. Well," he amended, "we will when my brilliant and powerful sorceress queen makes sure of it."

"You put a lot of faith in me."

"Yes," he replied, in that implacable tone. "And in me. Because, my lovely Oria, I no longer believe in the impossible. I've already seen it shattered. So, I do believe that, while it may not be easy, you and I will find a way to be husband and wife in truth. We will put you on the throne of Bára, save the Destrye, and go on to live long and happy lives, with many copper-haired children to dote us on us in our old age."

"And the drought? Will you also command the monsoons to return?"

"Of course not. That's your job. Mine is to keep you safe while you work your sorcery."

She had to laugh. "Not to mention tending my hair."

"It's like silk—and now it's all kinked from being in those braids, so each little bump catches the light. I'm torn on whether your *beah* should be plaited copper or smooth like when your hair is straight."

"A grave dilemma indeed."

"Very much so. I will have to see your hair both ways, many times before I can make such an important decision. I've discovered that's what being king mainly involves—making good decisions." His breath whispered over her ear again. "I intend to make very good ones with you, Oria, which means I'll tend you with great diligence."

Despite herself, she giggled at this playful side of him. "Well thank you for this. I do feel better having the braids out."

"You're welcome. Want to do me a favor in return?"

~ 10 ~

HE ALMOST REGRETTED asking the question, because she stiffened warily. Not, however, as much as she would have even a short time before, so he was making inroads on earning her trust. Maybe enough to push her a little further. And, if he hadn't gotten as far as he hoped, how she responded to this request would let him know where the boundaries lay. All the better to strategize how to shift them.

"Want me to brush your hair in return?" she asked, in that prim voice that told him she didn't want him to know how she felt.

He laughed. "Spoken like a person with straight hair. I have to use a comb on mine, with lots and lots of oil."

"I know how to use a comb, Lonen."

"All right, then that would be welcome." In fact, he might greatly enjoy having her tend him in turn. "But that's not what I'm asking for right now."

"What then?" she prompted, with some impatience. Wanting to get it over with, perhaps, and clearly suspicious.

He put his lips close to the delicate curve of her ear. She shivered so deliciously when he murmured into it that he couldn't wait to experience her response when he licked her there. And elsewhere.

"I'd like to see you naked," he murmured.

As he expected, she tried to pull away, but didn't get far with his hand firmly wrapped in her hair. "Don't fly away, Oria. I'm just asking. You can say no."

"I'm saying no." But she was breathless, a high blush on her fair cheekbones. "Let me go."

"As my queen commands." He released her hair with some regret, already missing the silky mass of it sliding through his hands. Oria immediately leapt away, putting several feet between her and the bed. To his good fortune, in her haste she also forgot that the bright sunshine from the terrace silhouetted her slender form in the thin silk gown, her hair a shining cape around her. He folded his hands behind his neck, preparing for whatever lecture she intended to deliver, and enjoying the view in the meanwhile. Particularly the enticing triangle between her shapely thighs.

"Why?" she demanded.

He dragged his gaze back up to her face, though he couldn't read much of her expression with the light behind her. "I already told you."

She threw up her hands in exasperation. "And you think this will make you happy, being able to see me naked and not being able to do anything about it."

"I wouldn't agree I can't do anything about it."

"Sometimes you seem so smart and then you constantly forget that—"

"I haven't forgotten," he stopped her there, sharply. "Enough of trying to make it seem that way. Seeing you will give me something to picture when I use my own fist for relief."

She went so still that he dearly wished to get a glimpse of her expression, but moving to see better might startle her.

"I have absolutely no idea how to respond to that," she

finally said, her tone faint.

"What shocks you—that I'd use my own hand in lieu of being inside you, or that I want the image of my naked wife to fantasize to while I do it?" That triangle between her thighs drew his eyes again. He could almost make out the division of her sex.

"Both, I think." Her voice was hushed. The silence drew out. "You're looking at my silhouette again, aren't you?"

"Oh yes," he replied, pushing the image forward so she might pick it up. "See yourself in my head?"

"I already look naked."

"Almost. The real thing would be better."

"I don't know." But she wavered, one hand tugging on the ties of her neckline. "I'm not sure how to feel about you picturing me while you…"

He waited but she didn't continue. "It seems wrong to picture anyone *but* you," he argued. Maybe another push. "You don't want me imagining Natly, do you?"

"A low blow there, Destrye." She moved out of the light, coming around to his side of the bed. At least he could see her face again, and the pink blush of her nipples. The shadow at her mound—not clear if her hair there was copper, too. He needed to know with a near-desperate thirst. His cock throbbed, so erect she had to be able to see the outline through the sheet. Indeed, her gaze did go there before she yanked it away. Tempting to take himself in hand and demonstrate to her then and there.

"Would you like to see it?" He asked.

Her coppery eyes flew wide and alarmed to his face. "No! I mean, not yet, I think."

Definite progress.

"Don't you do that, use your own hand, to pleasure yourself?"

She blushed nearly crimson. "I'm not having this conversation with you."

And yet she hadn't run. She lingered, curious and drawn despite herself. "You're already having this conversation," he pointed out. "And if we'd had a normal wedding night, we would have seen and done much more with each other."

"I haven't," she said abruptly, almost defiant. "Done that. *Normally* I don't feel the urge."

"Not ever?" He was flabbergasted.

"I don't think women do," she informed him coolly. "I'm not sure all men do."

"Oh, they do," he assured her. "Believe me, almost all men *and* women do."

She put her hands on her hips, delineating her narrow waist nicely. "You don't know that."

He considered it. "Yes, I do."

"Maybe the Destrye do it."

"You Bárans might have sticks up your asses, but I'm willing to bet money even your people do it.

She actually stomped her slender bare foot, forcing him to repress a smile. "I cannot believe you just said that to me!"

"Don't be annoyed. Having things up your ass can feel very nice. I'll show you."

She grabbed a pillow and flung it at his face with an incoherent screech. He caught it in time, but could no longer hold back the laughter. By the time he wiped the tears away, she'd composed herself, standing with folded arms, tapping her foot with barely contained ire.

"I was going to let you see me naked," she informed him coolly, "but not now."

She was killing him. "Aw, don't be that way. That's not

fair."

"Yes, it is." She lifted her pert chin and sniffed, as if she smelled something bad. "You don't deserve a treat like the sight of my naked body, not behaving like a barbarian."

Wait. She was actually teasing him. She looked perfectly composed, even disdainful, but something about her made him realize she was being playful. If only he could toss her on the bed and torment her into showing it. "Oria, I *am* a barbarian."

"So you've demonstrated," she retorted. "But you don't have to look like one. Come and sit. I'll comb your hair."

"Are you sure you won't—"

"Not happening." She turned crisply, hair crackling about her. "And I'm summoning Juli, so you might do something about *that*."

To his utter shock, something briefly grasped his cock, a shimmer of energy like a tiny bolt of lightning. "Arill!" he gasped, fighting not to spill his seed immediately like some oversexed adolescent.

Oria turned and flashed him a coy smile. "No, Destrye. That was me."

As SOON AS Lonen disappeared into her private bathing room— even before sending for Juli—Oria pulled a fresh set of priestess robes from the clothespress, hastily changed her chemise, and scrambled into the far more modest clothing. No more temptation, for either of them. She picked up her mask, wanting the comfort of its obscuring help, too, but the way Lonen had asked that she not... Well, she'd apparently developed a soft spot for the Destrye king because she set the mask aside again. She seemed to have a great deal of difficulty refusing him his requests, no matter how far she strayed from her usual behavior. A dangerous sign.

Especially that lapse in using grien on him. And sexually! Really, she couldn't imagine what had gotten into her, except that it had been so satisfying to see the look on Lonen's face. Plus she'd had to do something to vent all that sensual energy she'd absorbed. He deserved it, too, teasing her so mercilessly, making her lose all semblance of *hwil*. He'd so thoroughly seduced her that she'd been on the verge of dropping her chemise and demanding he show her how he pleasured himself.

Don't you do that, use your own hand, to pleasure yourself?

The question burned in her brain. Was it true that everyone else did that? Something she really didn't want to envision, the people she knew and loved, doing... No. Banishing that line of thought.

She really shouldn't have teased him, not the least because no one could know that she could use active grien that way. Stupid and impulsive. Of course Lonen wouldn't know the difference, but he might slip up and say the wrong thing, betraying her secret. But making sure he knew enough not to meant having to explain in the first place and she really wasn't at all sure that was wise. He might be insisting that their marriage was a real partnership, but only the day before he'd called her an enemy.

He talked of wedding dances, but they truly danced along a very thin line, each of them on opposite sides of it. She needed to keep that firmly in mind—and not fall into his flirtatious games.

She couldn't imagine what had gotten into her.

A scuffing sound alerted her to his approach. He emerged dressed in his Destrye clothing again. The animal skins had been dyed dark, as all the Destrye warriors seemed to wear. Was that for war or did they never dress in colors at all? Even his shirt woven of some plant material looked nearly black in the shadowed interior. At least the leather pants did more to conceal his flagrant manhood than the Báran silk trousers did. Though, judging by his relaxed and pleased expression, that might be because he'd relieved himself while in there. Something else she didn't want to know.

"You're blushing," he commented.

"It's warm in here."

"Especially for you with those layers of robes on."

As those layers formed at least a meager defense against his seductive ways, she had no intention of taking them off again. "Sit here if you want me to fix your hair."

Lonen sat in the chair before her, then leaned closer to examine the mirror, tapping it with a curious finger. "I've never seen such a thing. Like perfectly still lake water."

"Which I've never seen. It's more glass, treated with a liquid metal on one side, so it reflects."

He sat back in the chair with an amused grunt, shifting his study of the mirror itself to her, his gray eyes intent on hers. She concentrated on pouring some oil into her palm, so her curiosity wouldn't lead her to peeking into his thoughts. Careful not to touch his scalp, she brushed her oiled palms over his curls. They were softer than they looked, though coarser than her own hair. And intriguingly exotic. Still, it made no sense that it gave her pleasure to comb her fingers through them.

"Juli is having food sent up so we can breakfast here in the garden. We do have meat for you. The council session might last a long time, so you'd be wise to eat heartily."

"Fattening me up?"

He was too thin, it was true. Thinner than he'd been before and the guilt chewed at her, thinking of the Trom burning their crops. "I'd like to visit my mother beforehand, try to persuade her to attend. This is her plan as much as anyone's. Hopefully once she sees we're married, she'll relent and accept the reality of it."

"It's something she'll be able to know, just by looking at us?"

The man thought in questions. But he knew some of this already, so it wouldn't be telling him something new. Still, each secret revealed seemed to open the windows to a dozen more, making it more and more difficult to determine where to draw her boundaries with him. That thin line. "With sgath, yes. That's how I see with my mask on."

"What's that like?" He asked it easily enough, but his eyes met hers in the mirror, that obstinate challenge in them.

"I don't know how to explain it. Don't smirk. I was thinking how to describe it." She rapped him on the scalp with the glass comb.

"Ow."

"See? The sand is blowing in your tower now."

"Fair enough." He grinned at her. "I'd like to blow more than sand in your tower, Oria."

"You're incorrigible."

He sighed, trying to look sorrowful, but his playfully sexual thoughts tugged at her. "So my mother always says."

She resisted. "Is your mother alive?"

"Uh-uh. Not letting you distract me with questions. You were thinking about how to describe seeing with sgath to me. Is that related to the moon, Sgatha?"

"Yes. We believe Sgatha governs the flow of sgath." She drew the comb gently through his tangled curls, then closed her eyes to see it with sgath. "It's like ... like everything radiates a kind of light. Your hair looks different than your skin, and my hands look a different color from those. Even the comb has a little glow."

"Juli said magic comes from life, but the comb isn't alive."

Opening her eyes, she looked at him in the mirror. "It is, just not in the way you think of it. Everything has energy to it. This comb, like the mirror, are both made of sand, melted and transformed, but which used to be part of the ocean. They carry a kind of ... memory of what they once were."

He frowned. "That makes no sense."

"I told you it was hard to explain."

"I know, I know—don't get all huffy. Go on."

She pulled at the curls a little harder than she needed to, but he didn't wince. "That's all there is to tell."

"Liar," he mocked, softly.

"Ask me questions then, which you're so brilliant at anyway."

He didn't even have to pause to think. "So, everyone who wears a mask can see with this sgath?"

"The priestesses," she corrected. It wouldn't do for him to insult a Báran priest by suggesting he used sgath. "The priests use grien."

"Governed by Grienon."

"There you go."

"And does grien work the same way?"

Shifting sands here. "I don't know, as I'm not a man."

He grinned, vividly picturing her standing in her chemise in the light. "Now that is a truth."

His curls reasonably tamed and oiled, she went to fetch the

leather tie he'd left on the table by the bed. She handed it to him, not certain she could gather the springy stuff together well enough without risking touching his skin. He didn't take it, however. Instead he picked up a long lock of her hair where it streamed over her shoulder and coiled it around his finger. "What is it you're not telling me?"

"Besides centuries of secret temple knowledge? I can't imagine."

He tugged on her hair. "Your sarcasm makes me makes me want to toss you on that bed until you're too delirious with pleasure to think straight."

That made her head reel right there. "I had to marry a Destrye with an enormous idea of himself."

"That's not the only thing that's enormous. You'll find out someday and then I'll accept *that* apology when you tell me how wrong you were."

"Ha!" She tried to step back, but he held on, his eyes turning somber.

"Oria—I can't be your partner in this if you keep me blind and deaf. There's something there, about sgath and grien that you're not telling me."

She pulled at the leather tie, tugging it between her fingers as she'd been in the habit of doing since Lonen had left it behind. How was he reading into her? She'd faked *hwil* well enough to fool the High Priestess, she certainly should be able to hide a lie from a mind-dead foreigner. "I'm not keeping you blind and deaf. I can't imagine what makes you think I am."

No longer soft, the gray of his eyes went flinty, looking more like the granite she'd first thought of when she saw him full of battle fury and spattered with blood at the city gates. "I don't know what it is either, but it's like there's part of you in me now. Maybe you gave me some of your magic."

"That's not possible." *Was it?*

"I really hate it when you tell me something's impossible, Oria."

"Then you're in for long years of misery, because someone has to be practical in this marriage."

"You said the magic ritual bound us together," he flung back at her. "Magic. Connection. You. Me. I'm in you and you're in me. And I know when you're lying to me. Another ground rule for you—I also hate it when you lie to me."

She struggled with her rising anger and all the emotion he emanated. Too much input from him, on top of all that had gone the night before, no matter how much better she'd done. She might be faking *hwil* most of the time, but it still took a measure of equanimity to do that much. Not a state of mind being around Lonen helped her to achieve. Terrible timing, when she couldn't afford any apparent lapse of *hwil* before confronting the council. Even as she wrestled both his emotional energy and hers, the marginal control she managed eroded like sand slipping through her fingers.

She needed Chuffta and he wasn't there.

"I'm coming back. Stay steady."

Could it be some of the Destrye was in her? That would explain her uncharacteristically salacious behavior. But she had too much grien in her already—she couldn't afford to have even more. Lonen waited her out, holding her leashed by the lock of her hair, implacable, though his thumb absently stroked over it.

She took a steadying breath. "You don't listen well. There are things you can't know. That would be beyond dangerous to me to reveal to you."

He didn't like it, his brows lowering and some of that dark
r brooding in the background of his thoughts. "I wouldn't

do anything to endanger you, Oria."

"You wouldn't mean to, no." She slapped the tie on the table, snagged a ribbon knife, and neatly cut of the lock of hair he held—then swiftly made good her escape. "But as both our peoples have amply demonstrated, we don't have to set out with the intention of harming each other in order to do it in grand fashion."

"It's hardly the same thing," he nearly growled.

She pointed at him. "Destrye." Then tapped her breast. "Báran. It's exactly the same thing." She turned to go.

"We're not done talking, Oria." Some of his frustrated anger snaked around her, adding to the uneven charge already building. Hopefully Chuffta would return soon. She desperately needed to vent.

"You want to be my partner? Use that anger to help me get the council to ratify me as queen. That's why we got married in the first place, not to loll in bed all morning and play sexy games. This is a marriage of state and so it will remain. We both have grave responsibilities to our peoples and you'd do well to remember that, King Lonen."

~ 11 ~

H E NEARLY LUNGED after her. Stopped himself by dint of will that had carried him through battles that stronger men than he had fallen to. How had things between them deteriorated so swiftly? All he knew was he'd undone everything he'd built.

No, *she* had cut the fragile ties of trust they'd been creating, snicking it to pieces with her little silver knife.

She might as well have plunged it into his heart. Walking away from him with that chill in her gaze, leaving only a shining lock of her copper hair behind. Metal could be cold, too. He'd do well to remember that in dealing with her.

Forcing himself to keep to a walk, he tucked the lock of hair in his pocket, and then his hands. An extra measure to ensure he didn't forget himself and touch her. Or throttle her.

He sauntered onto the terrace, scanning it. The brightly colored silk banners that provided shade hung lax in the still air, the brilliant blossoms of fabulous flowers likewise hanging off draping vines, trees and stalks. The ones that hadn't dried to brown crisps drooped, wilting in the sun. A low drone hummed around him, like heat given sound. No, it came from insects buzzing around the blooms and small birds, moving so fast as they dipped from plant to plant that their wings became a blur. The jewelbirds.

Not in the shade as a reasonable person would be, Oria instead stood in one of her habitual positions, over by the stone balustrade, gazing out at the city and the sere plains beyond. The sun glinted off her cape of hair, like the hammered copper drums of the Destrye.

She dazzled him. Seduced and infuriated him. All thoughts led to the sorceress. She'd well and truly bewitched him and yet cared nothing for him except as a player in her plans.

He was an idiot to have married her.

"You only have to put up with me a few days more," she said, still in that imperiously cool tone and not in the way he found irresistibly desirable either. "Then you can go home and be free of me."

He hadn't meant to be thinking that so loudly. "Not true," he countered with ill grace. "We will never be free of each other."

"You will be free of my immediate presence," she amended, with such equanimity that he brought up some lurid thoughts about her, just to shake her up.

"Stop that."

"Why should I? And don't you dare lecture me on my responsibilities to my people. I came here for them. Married *you*, for them. You're not the only one making sacrifices here."

"I never imagined I was," she gritted through clenched teeth.

There—not so cool and remote. *You radiate emotional energy as fierce as the sun's heat in summer.* By Arill, he'd use that to thaw her, make her deal with him as a partner, if not her equal. Barbarian and mind-dead he might be, but irresponsible ruler he wasn't. "I think you do imagine that," he taunted her.

Oria refused to look at him, but her fingers flexed on the railing. Apparently she did that a great deal because she'd worn the gritty stone smooth in places, always up in her lonely tower, secluded from the world.

"Princess Oria, all alone in her quiet world, with her flowers, her jewelbirds, and her Familiar. Well, I have news for you. You're no longer alone. You don't get to be. I'm your husband and you will not shut me out. Not out of your ambitions. Not out of your emotions." He leaned in, letting her feel all the heated desire she stirred in him. "And not out of your bed."

"Stop doing that!" She scanned the sky, looking for that pet lizard she liked so well, no doubt.

"Why should I?" he repeated the question, ruthlessly pushing her.

"Because." She rounded on him at last, face flushed from fury, the heat, or both. "You want to know a secret? Fine. Here's one for you. To receive a mask, we have to prove that we've achieved *hwil*."

"Like your golems and your blank masks," he sneered. "Creatures devoid of feeling."

"If only," she snapped back. "You wanted to know so badly what it is? Well ask some other priestess because I've never achieved *hwil*. That's right, I faked it, with my mother's help. And if they find out, they'll take my mask away, and I will never become queen. So wrap your clever brain around that concept and stop trying to get to me emotionally." Her breath caught, nearly a sob. "If you won't do it for my sake, then do it for your people. Because you're going to destroy us all for the sake of your cursed male pride."

"Oria." He caught the sleeve of her robe as she turned away again. He was an ass. "Hey. I didn't know. I can't know these things unless you let me in on these secrets. That's my whole point."

"Well now you do. There: one more in my vast array of flaws." She wiped furiously at her cheeks. "You wanted into my feelings? Here I am, a whole boggy, bloody mess of them."

Oria's sensitivity ... both her blessing and her curse.

"I don't believe you're flawed."

"What do you know of it, Destrye?" She demanded, all Báran princess at her imperious best.

He held onto his patience by a thin thread, the sun hot on his oiled hair that she'd tended with such care. A mercurial woman, restless and changeable, his sorceress wife. "Obviously not a whole lot, since you refuse to explain it to me."

She didn't reply, pressing her lips against whatever tart—or wounded—reply she'd had on the tip of her tongue. Then she gave a glad cry as Chuffta winged up, landing on the balustrade with a scrabble of talons on stone. Wings still spread, he balanced as he snaked his long neck against her throat, letting her embrace him, running slim fingers over his shining white scales.

Lonen was in a hell of his own making that he'd be fighting sick jealousy over her love for the dragonlet. His fingers itched to grab his axe and chop something up. Oria, for example. In fact, maybe he should work off some of that energy. It could only help both of them.

Leaving them to their little love fest, he went inside long enough to strip to his small clothes and grab his axe, then found another spot on her expansive terrace and set to running strengthening exercises. His muscles responded stiffly at first— the wages of too little exercise the past days of riding to Bára and negotiations and rituals—but gradually they warmed.

His faithful battle axe felt good in his grip, reassuring, steady, and real. The opposite of magic in its inert iron. That was something that wasn't alive in any way. A flaw in Oria's assertions. He ran the drills with the axe in his right hand, then switched to the left. The wise warrior prepared for all eventualities.

By the time he felt like he could operate out of a place of calm logic instead of unreasoning, jealous anger, he dripped sweat. He had to use Oria's private bathing chamber to wash off again, which only made him think again about coming in his own fist earlier, dazzling images of Oria in his head.

All thoughts led to the sorceress.

At least able to behave like a civilized man again, he found Oria in the shade of her silk sail in the seats by her fire table, though it was only smooth creamy stone, no dancing violet flames. A good thing, as a number of plates of food and pitchers sat there instead. Juli had done her mistress's hair up in the complex braids again, and Oria now wore a more elaborate set of the crimson priestess robes, kind of a cross between one of her royal gowns and the daily robes. Chuffta sat beside her, tail wrapped around her wrist like a series of bracelets. And, of course, Arill take her—she wore her cursed mask again.

He fingered the lock of her hair in his pocket. She hadn't intended it as a gift, obviously, but he'd keep it as such, having found a few pieces of cut ribbon to bind each end.

"How are you feeling?" he asked, not sure how else to open the next phase of conversation.

"I won't fall apart in the next moments, at any rate." She stroked Chuffta's wing and the derkesthai gazed at him, green eyes full of intelligence, but no accusation that he could detect.

"Master Chuffta," he greeted the Familiar as Juli had, then offered one used by the Destrye. "Did you enjoy good hunting?"

Chuffta blinked and dipped his chin, looking pleased indeed. Oria made a little sound of surprise.

"What?"

"He didn't say anything to me, just communicated directly to you. He doesn't usually do that."

Lonen sat, using a pair of glass picks to stab a piece of meat. Could be filling his griping stomach would help his mood immensely. "Probably Chuffta knows that he and I are in this together with you, so we might as well find ways to communicate with each other besides through you."

"Don't start." She sounded weary, but he couldn't let her off this climbing rope while they still dangled so far above ground.

"I'm not. I'm continuing. You and I have things to sort out before we walk into that council chamber, in order to be a cohesive fighting unit. If only to serve our grave responsibilities to our peoples."

She sighed, a rough, injured sound that grabbed at his heart. "I suppose I deserve that. But you push me, Lonen. You push and push and…" She finished on another empty breath, then filled a glass with juice, her hand shaking. Belatedly she seemed to realize she couldn't drink with her mask on and sat there, holding it.

"Here, let me help you take it off." He rose and walked behind her.

"You don't have to—"

"I might as well learn the tricks of it, right? Something I can do for you when it's just the two of us, so you don't have to call on Juli every time."

"Fine." He imagined she rolled her eyes, which was better than the defeated attitude. "There's a knife—"

"I've already found the knots and can get them." They were tucked in among the braids, cleverly hidden, but not that difficult to undo.

"You interrupt me a lot."

He opened his mouth to retort, but realized that she had a point. "You're right. I'm an impatient brute. I'll try to do better."

She held the mask in place as he worked. "Not entirely impatient. You seem to be good with knots."

A peace offering? He'd take it. "I've worked with rope a lot. Climbing trees, cliffs, that kind of thing."

"City walls," she said in a more pointed voice. So much for peace.

"Weren't you the one who said we needed to get past accusations and apologies over with?" He finished with the third set of ribbons and slipped the mask from her hands, setting it on the tile kept for it nearby. Uncovering the bowl next to it, he found one of her damp and freshly scented cloths inside and offered it to her.

Eyes flashing up to him in surprise, she took the cloth, mopping her flushed face with it. Her eyes were red and swollen from crying, which meant the few tears he'd witnessed hadn't been the end of it. Giving her a moment to compose herself, he sat again, spearing more meat.

"You're supposed to use them like this." Oria picked up a pair and demonstrated holding them both in one hand, deftly plucking a grape from a platter.

He studied her hold, emulated it and tried the same with a piece of meat. Easier to learn on that than on something slippery like a grape. On his second try he got it and Oria smiled at him. A real one, if sad. "You're good with your hands in many ways."

Not the time to tease her with the sexual remark that sprang to mind at that. "I guess so? I've always liked doing things with my hands—wood carving and such." He set down the eating picks and studied his hands. "I don't like that they give you pain."

She took a breath. "It's not pain, exactly."

"Okay." He waited, restraining the questions that annoyed her so. Instead he piled a plate with a bunch of leaves, grass, and sticks—or whatever in Arill it all was—and handed it to her. When she stared at it with a blank expression, he nudged it a little. "Eat. Long council session, remember. You don't eat enough."

"I feel guilty," she admitted, balancing the plate on her knees, sharp under the silk, and poked at the greens. "I keep thinking what it takes to grow this and where we stole the water from."

"It seems to me that you spend too much time feeling guilty about things that aren't your fault and you can't control."

"For someone who claims to want to know me better and be my partner, you criticize me an awful lot."

"It's not criticism—it's good advice. You can't lead your people to better lives if you're not strong. There's no sense in starving yourself to make up for the past."

"Is that why you've lost so much weight?" she retorted. "Because you've been eating so well, so you can be strong to lead your people?"

"Point taken. But in truth it wasn't guilt that stopped me so much as lack of opportunity and appetite for the options I had. Don't apologize for that either. You eat and I'll get us back on topic. It seems to me, as we were discussing earlier, that your sensitivity to emotional energy is also what gives you powerful magic. Juli called it your blessing and curse together."

"Juli talks too much," she muttered, but she speared up

some greens and chewed. When she swallowed, she pointed the glass picks at him. "And I'm not that powerful. I'm still figuring things out. The magic is strong sometimes, but it's also hard to … direct."

He nodded thoughtfully, grabbing a platter of cheese and scooping some onto her plate. "So, you're like a young warrior after a big growth spurt. You don't know where your body is or how to make your size and strength work for you. You're learning to swing the magical equivalent of a sword, but right now you're your own worst enemy because you keep hitting your own self in the noggin with it."

She gave him a funny look. "That actually makes a weird kind of sense."

"I don't know much about magic, but I do know something about training young men—well, people—in using their Arill-bestowed gifts. Just because she gave it to you, doesn't mean you don't have to practice diligently to hone those talents into something you can actually wield with confidence. Natural born talent only gets you ten percent there. Hard work and refining your skills is the rest of the battle."

She was quiet a moment, thankfully eating with more enthusiasm. "You're never quite what I expect," she finally said.

He grunted a laugh. "Good. As you're never what I expect either. We're a perfect match."

"We're not, though." She gazed at him somberly, eyes dark with concern. "And the council will know it. Worse news is, my mother refuses to see me. Her attendants say she was so upset about my—our—marriage when I sent a message to her that she said all sorts of horrible things, then fell into a fugue state."

"I'm sorry." He couldn't imagine how that would be,

though if those servants were his, he'd take them to task for passing along the ranting of a madwoman. That did no one any good. "You know that, whatever she said, she didn't mean it. You said yourself she's not in her right mind."

"I know that in my head." Oria glanced at her Familiar and rolled her shoulders. "The point is, she won't be helping."

"We'll do it ourselves then." He scooped some stuff onto her plate that looked unfortunately like maggots. Hopefully it wasn't really, but if it was... well, good protein. Maybe he could eventually talk her into eating meat. That would help fill out those waifish hollows around her collarbones.

"I don't think I can do it." She nearly whispered the words, then glanced down at Chuffta, who gazed up at her with an intent green gaze.

Practicing being the better man, Lonen gave them a few minutes to converse, using the opportunity to devour more of the really excellent meat. Some kind of venison, maybe. And there were pieces of fowl with a spicy seasoning he really enjoyed.

"Want to loop me in?" he finally asked and Oria looked over at him with a flush on her cheekbones.

"Mostly Chuffta is telling me the same things you are, that I should share more with you and trust you to help me with the council."

Surprisingly honored, he dipped his chin at her Familiar. "Good man."

Oria rolled her eyes at them both and threw up her hands, which seemed a good sign indeed. Fiesty Oria would be far better at his side than the dejected one. "Fine. I can't believe I'm going to do this. But I need to swear you to secrecy somehow. Vow to your goddess or something."

He considered her. The vow waited to be made, of course.

Would have been already, had they married in Arill's temple according to Destrye custom. By altering the words slightly, they could fit his and Oria's unusual union. A risk, promising so much to her, and yet... he was already committed, wasn't he? They both were.

As he'd said to her the evening before, he'd already made the decision, and he wasn't a man to go back on that. No matter his other flaws.

He set his plate aside, going to one knee before her. In the old tradition, he picked up the hem of her silk robe, kissed it, then caught and held her gaze. "I swear by the magic that binds us, by the seed of me in you and the blossom of you in me, that I shall never betray you, my wife, whether by action or inaction."

She stared at him, lips parted, pink with the fruit she'd eaten. If only he could taste her, let her taste him, they'd be so much easier with each other. Of her own accord, she lifted a hand and carefully tucked one of his escaped curls into his tied-back hair. "Thank you," she said, seeming both moved and chastened.

Tempted to break the tension with a joke, he resisted the urge. This was an important moment between them. "We both have fealties, Oria, people to whom we owe our allegiance, but we can be united in that. Trust me to help you."

"All right," she breathed. For a moment she seemed about to touch him, but she caught herself and shooed him away. "Go sit over there. You're too close for me to keep my head straight."

He let himself grin at her then. It salved his admittedly too-large masculine pride that he affected her as much she did him. Doing as she asked, he added more food to her plate, then to his own. She shook her head at him. "This is more food than

I've eaten in weeks."

"Good. Maybe you'll start making up for senselessly depriving yourself. Now, tell me what I need to know."

Putting her eating picks together, she used them as a platform to lift the maggoty things to her mouth. They didn't move, so maybe they're weren't insect larvae after all.

"This is the thing. You asked me what the Trom said to me that day, why its touch didn't kill me." She gazed at him steadily, no waffling now, but studying his reactions, probably reading his emotions, too, so he kept his mind calm and still as the lakes of Dru. "It called me Princess *Ponen*, which my mother—during a fortuitous lucid period—explained is a very old word that means powerful potential."

She set her plate aside and scrubbed her palms over her knees, probably unaware that she left sweat marks from them. The memory bothered her far more than she wanted to let on.

"What it turns out to mean for me is that I have both sgath and grien." She lifted her chin, daring him to comment.

"So you have the male kind of magic, too."

"Yes." She waited, maybe for him to be horrified or something, but he kept to the placid lake image. No judgment from him. If that made her more powerful, all the better for the Destrye. "You have to understand," she continued, her face very serious. "Sgath is passive. Priestesses absorb magic, we gather and pool it, then feed it to our priests. *They* make it active, using grien to build things."

"Or make earthquakes and fireballs to destroy things," he noted wryly, then regretted breaking his own rule about not referencing past wrongs. She didn't seem to notice, however.

"Exactly. It's … beyond unseemly for a woman to be able to wield grien. It's anathema. If anyone finds out, they won't just take my mask and deny me the throne, they'll execute me."

Something hard and mean stirred in him at that. "They'd have to go through me."

She gazed at him in momentary astonishment. "I don't think you—"

"It's not a matter of debate, and I'm sorry I interrupted you again, but I'm not going to argue about this. If any of those red-robed golem wannabes make a move to lay a finger on you, I'll burn down Bára before I let that happen." The anger felt good. She wanted him to channel it? There it was. "You're mine now, Oria, which means I'll protect you with the last breath in my body."

"What about your responsibility to the Destrye?" she challenged.

"Don't give me that. You're my queen now and the best hope of saving my people. My loyalty is one and the same. I'll wield my axe for you as I would for them."

"Some things can't be resolved with brute strength." Her eyes flashed as she said it and he began to see the sides of her she'd described. Both the sensitivity that allowed her to read his thoughts, feel his emotions, and even absorb some of those energies, and also the direct ferocity in her restless nature, the courage and willingness to fight.

"I know that," he replied calmly. "That's why I came to you, after all."

"I thought you came to me with the intention of throttling me for supposedly breaking my word to you." She said it with the same tone of challenge, but a hint of mischief lurked in her composed expression.

"A good warrior is ready for all eventualities—back up plans are key."

"A salient point, as we need one for the council session, in case things go awry."

"Sound reasoning. Are the three of us the only ones who know about the grien in you?"

Looking thoughtful, she scratched her Familiar's breast, who seemed to be for all the world, smiling at him. A strange sight on a lizard's face. "Chuffta will never tell. But there's also my mother."

"Who loves you and would never put you in jeopardy, even if she's upset about this marriage."

"Hopefully, unless she gets it in her head that she's helping somehow, in her fugue state. She's not the greatest danger, however." Oria grimaced apologetically. "Yar might guess."

~ 12 ~

"YAR?" Lonen knew he must be gaping at her, but … "Yar? As in your brother who's battling you for the throne and can be expected to use any and all weapons against you to win—that Yar?"

"It's not like there are others," she bit out and stood, picking up her mask.

He held out a hand for it and she sighed, coming to sit beside him, giving it to him. He studied the pattern of the braids, looking for places to weave the ribbons back in. Maybe he could learn to do the braids also, if she insisted on keeping them, so he could take her hair down as often as he liked, then help her get ready for public appearances, too.

"As zealously as you guard this secret," he said, "I'm assuming you did not confide in him."

"No. Not at all. In fact—I didn't know I had grien magic until a confrontation with him."

"A confrontation?" He kept his voice neutral, focusing on making the ribbons tight enough to hold the mask on, but not make her uncomfortable. She must have washed her hair, too, while he was working off his mad, because she smelled of a different flower now. And he should have killed that officious twerp when he had the chance.

"Don't think I can't detect those thoughts beneath that pretty mountain lake and musing about my hair. It's honeysuckle and, yes, Yar and I had a fight and I attacked him with my grien magic. He ran away. It's over. I defended myself and won, so you can forget about those revenge fantasies you're brewing."

"The lakes of Dru are very beautiful, lovely to swim in during the hot summer months. I'll take you to my favorite." His favorite that still existed, as the first two were nothing but holes in the ground, but he wouldn't burden her with that guilt as well.

"I don't know how to swim." She sounded bemused.

The ribbons took a lot longer to weave in than to undo. "You don't?"

"I've never seen enough water in one place to be able to swim in it. The baths are as deep as it gets around here."

"What about the bay?"

She shook her head minutely, so as not to disturb his work. "Outside the city walls, remember?"

"So what's up with that aspect—what does it do to you to go outside them?"

"You saw." She made a disgusted sound. "I don't know how it works, but somehow the city walls shield the priestesses. They allow us to focus on the sgath beneath Bára, to absorb what's described as a concentrated, clean magic, rather than the chaotic variety in the outer world. Outside, we kind of overload."

"Just as you do with skin-to-skin contact with someone who's not shielded with *hwil*."

"You do pay attention."

"And here you say I don't listen. So I'm also thinking this is why the priestesses were on the walls for the battle—because they can't go past them."

"That and the source of magic is below Bára and we can't go far from it."

"You said sgath comes from Sgatha."

"It does, but via her communion with the earth. Bára sits on a special place—as do our sister cities—where the sgath filters through the rocks and soil, becoming harmonized in a way, so that we can take it in without damage. We have to learn to do that judiciously, so we don't overload."

"Thus your high lonely tower."

"Thus my high, peaceful, and quiet tower, yes."

He let that go. "But you can't use this chaotic magic in the greater world that you mentioned?" Two ribbons down, one more to go. The intricate task helped him order his thoughts and questions.

"I think it's like trying to light a candle with a lightning bolt. But nobody tries, that I know of, because we can't leave the sgath provided by our cities."

"What happens if you do?"

"What happens to a plant without water?"

A too apt analogy, sitting in her dying garden. She hadn't been exaggerating about the impact of her trying to go to Dru. Ah well, that road lay over the next rise.

"So, Yar might guess and would surely use this knowledge to undermine your bid for the throne, but he's not here. Do you think he told anyone?"

"I don't think so—it would be to his advantage to keep the knowledge to himself. Also, I can't see the temple not acting on it if he told anyone there, and I'm clearly not dead. But I do think that's part of his hurry to find a bride. With an ideal partner, he'd have more than enough power to handle me. Failing that, he might try to expose me if I'm not crowned before he returns."

"Why not expose you after that point—get the temple to execute you and take the crown once you're gone?"

"The queen—or king—trumps the temple. They would not be able to act against me."

"All the more reason to succeed this afternoon then. There. All tightly masked again."

"Thank you." She adjusted to face him, but didn't move as far away as she might have once. "I know the mask repels you, so I appreciate your helping me with it."

Slowly, so she'd have time to stop him, he raised his hand and ran a fingertip along the cheekbone of the metallic face, just as he'd longed to do with her. "There's one advantage. At least I can touch this."

"You're obsessed with touching me," she said, but without her usual exasperation.

The metal was strangely cool, not as hot from the sun as he might have imagined. "I'm a man of the physical. Maybe I need to feel things to believe in them."

"Maybe I'm not real." A bit of whimsy from her, but also hints of darker pain beneath.

"Sometimes I wonder." Sometimes all of it seemed like a dream, that he might be still standing on that wall, blood dripping from his hands, while he glimpsed her, a vision from fantasy, candlelit in a window. He tapped the mask. "But this feels like it."

"And it allows me to fake *hwil*," she replied, all seriousness. "That's what you need to know if you're going to help me. If I lose that façade in the council session—and it's entirely possible because I'm already bursting with sgath and I can't vent to grien—then I'll lose all chance at being queen."

"So, you'd faint again?"

"Possibly. Or worse."

She meant exposing herself as a wielder of grien. "Maybe we should wait. Let you rest another day or two."

She wrung her hands together. "We can't afford the time. Yar could return at any moment."

"I don't like risking your health."

"That's not important."

"It is to me. It should be to you."

She waved that off, though Chuffta rustled his wings in a way that made him think the Familiar agreed. "I've survived similar crises so far. But I mean that the real worst case scenario is that I could accidentally use grien like I did with Yar," she said, confirming his speculation.

"Then you'd be forced to lay about with that battle axe of yours and that can't end well."

He smiled grimly for her little joke, but didn't let it distract him. "Then why not get rid of some on purpose now, before we go? Vent it like you say. Bleed off the energy."

She stood, scrubbing her hands together. "Because I'm afraid of hitting myself in the noggin with my own sword," she admitted ruefully. "Women aren't taught to control grien, only sgath. I have no idea what I'm doing. I've only ever used it impulsively, out of emotion, not *hwil*."

"You used it on me." The realization dawned on him. "You nearly made me come right there and then when you used it on my cock."

"Lonen!"

"Hey sorceress—you're the one who did it. I'm just talking about it."

"Is there nothing you won't give voice to?"

He pretended to think about it, then grinned at her. "No."

"Well, I shouldn't have done that." She gestured wildly,

crimson rippling in the breeze of her pacing. "It was irresponsible and impulsive and wrong. That's why it's really bad that I don't have real *hwil*. I could have hurt you."

"Felt amazing, in truth. Feel free to yank that particular chain any time you get the urge."

She stomped her foot, a gesture he was beginning to love. "This is a serious conversation."

"I'm always serious."

She paused her pacing, mask swinging to him in a posture of utter astonishment. "Liar," she said softly, exactly as he'd said it before.

He held up his palms in surrender, laughing. "Guilty."

"How can you laugh at a time like this?"

"It feels good to laugh. A kind of tension release, don't you think?" She didn't answer, simply tapped her foot, so he forged on. "In all seriousness, you have too much sgath and that pushes you to overload. Chuffta helps manage that, doesn't he?"

She considered him. "He does, yes—kind of like a buffer, but it only goes so far. Transforming the sgath to grien and releasing it, that feels best."

"So manly things would work to release it, huh? A good physical workout always helps me."

"I noticed," she replied in a dry tone.

"Did you—were you watching me earlier?" The thought pleased him immeasurably.

"I could hardly help it," she sniffed, but she resumed pacing.

"Did you like what you saw?"

"I saw you naked before," she pointed out. "In the baths."

"Doesn't answer the question."

"This is a pointless direction. It won't help me figure out a way to vent."

"I don't know." He stretched out his arms on the seat back. "A good orgasm always works for me that way. Very relaxing."

She actually clapped her hands over her ears. "I'm not hearing this."

"Yes, well—it's not a good solution anyway, since you won't pleasure yourself and I haven't completely determined how to give you a climax without touching you. I have ideas, but there's not enough time to implement them."

"Oh, I'm sorry—were you talking? I couldn't hear you."

She was wound up all right. Judging by the angle of the sun, they needed to begin the long descent from her tower soon, too. He mulled the problem.

How would he help the young warrior of his analogy?

ORIA SIMMERED MOLTEN as glass in a forge, running through with hot colors. At least Lonen wasn't deliberately provoking her any longer—not energetically anyway—which she had to admit was an excellent reason to have let him in on some of her weaknesses. She still felt unsettlingly exposed to have the Destrye know so much about her, but that vow he'd made her...

It had the force of magic, something she couldn't make sense of.

Especially with so much else on her mind.

"I have an idea." Lonen stood and came towards her, looking far too potent via sgath. In many ways, it was easier to look on him with her physical eyes. She perceived less of the coiling energies around him that so distracted her. She held up hands to fend him off and he darkened with displeasure. "Relax, I'm not going to do anything to you. I'll save that for tonight," he added, sensual energy snaking towards in that way that went right through her every time.

"There might be the coronation ceremony tonight," she reminded him, pointedly stepping back. "In fact, we'd better be hoping there is."

His naughty good humor faded. "What does that entail?"

"I don't know—I've never seen one."

"Will it be like the wedding ceremony, impacting you as badly?"

"Or worse. I really don't know, but we should be prepared for that eventuality."

He crackled with lashing impatience. "How can you not know these things?"

"The temple isn't exactly forthcoming with its secrets. And that's part of the test—if you know what's coming, a person can prepare for it."

"Seems being better prepared would ensure fewer failures."

She held up her palms, acknowledging the point. "Arguably, if we fail the temple's tests, then we can't be trusted with the power of the temple's secrets. If I can't survive the coronation ceremony, then I don't deserve to be queen."

He gazed at her a long moment. "And you call us a brutal people."

"There's all kinds of brutality in the world," she informed him softly.

"True." He shook it off, surveying her with the intent perspective of a warrior. Funny how he shifted so clearly to her sgath vision, from lover to king to fighter. "I've got an idea. Let's get at it this way. You had three brothers, all grien users. I know you spent a lot of time in your tower, but I also know what sisters are like. Surely you hung around them some, listening to them talk. Boys like to screw around with what they can do—did you ever watch them play fireballs versus earthquakes or anything like that?"

She nearly laughed at his phrasing, but…

"Yes!" A kaleidoscope of memories crashed through her. So many times that Ben, Nat, and Yar had argued over meals, boasting of their new tricks and challenging each other. She'd hated those conversations because of how left out she'd felt. Particularly after Ben, who'd been the last of her brothers to take the mask and thus her partner in being the slow student, had joined their ranks. But she'd also listened with the sick envy of someone who believed she'd never be as good as they were.

And Nat, back when she was younger, he'd entertained her by juggling fireballs. He'd spent weeks working up the trick—which meant a fair number of fireballs had gone astray. Then there was the time Yar widened a chasm to trip up Ben and nearly got them both killed. Father had been furious.

"Yes, they played games all right, but…" She hissed a little between her teeth, thinking about it. "I'm afraid I'll break something."

"That's the female in you talking."

"What?" Infuriated, she clenched her fists, wanting nothing more than to smash one into his easy, taunting mien.

"I'll let you in on a male secret, Oria. Boys, particularly younger ones who've just figured out that they have strength they didn't have before, don't think about what they might break. They just mess around and forget about consequences.

This is not always a good thing," he added, "which is why they need to be kept occupied and on a short leash by people who *are* aware of the consequences, but in this case I think the stakes are high enough that you should forget about breaking something."

"Young male derkesthai are the same. When they first come into their flames, no nest is safe."

She shook her head at Chuffta and relayed the words to Lonen.

He tossed a little salute to her Familiar. The interactive energy between them had changed, overlapping in interesting ways. Ones that she'd have to study later, at her leisure. Should that day ever come.

"Okay then," Lonen said. "So just let it go. Swing that sword and stop fretting."

"I'm not fretting."

"If you were a guy, I'd call you chicken. But I don't want to hurt your tender female feelings."

"Don't you taunt me, Destrye."

He pursed his lips and blew her a little kiss, a potent spark with it. "Chicken," he called.

It would serve him right if she let loose on him, but she still had little idea what affinity her grien would take, other than a kind of green fire, sometimes knocking things over, or stirring up dust devils. Still—female fretting or not—it seemed unwise to simply unleash all that sgath she'd built up into just any random manifestation of grien magic.

It would really help if she knew more about grien.

But there was something—a passing remark from one of her teachers who'd sought to reassure her about taking so long to master *hwil* and find her sgath. The priestess had said grien magic was easier to learn because it burgeoned in young men as part of their youthful vitality, pushing up like the sap in the trees in springtime. They had to practice restraint, focus, and release, while women's magic worked in the reverse. Instead of exploding outward, sgath drew in and received.

She had no time just then to learn restraint, focus, and release—but she knew something about trees and the sap rising in them. Looking around at her dying garden, it seemed she could hardly do more damage to it than withholding water had done.

"Okay, gentlemen, both of you get behind me. This could get messy."

Lonen didn't argue for once, moving quickly behind her with an aura of excited anticipation. Chuffta took wing, landing on the stone balustrade.

"Want me to be on you, instead?"

"No. I don't want to risk catching you in the backlash."

"This is fun."

"It's not fun, it's necessary."

"It can be both."

"This is going to be great," Lonen said.

Men.

"You know you love us."

Chuffta's smug reply tugged her in a funny way, but she screened that out, concentrating on her task. Using what little *hwil* that came to her easily, letting go of worry about her inadequate control—fretting, indeed!—she focused her mind on the trees in her garden, their crisping leaves and bare branches, the wilted blossoms and the husks of others littering the stones around them. It hurt her heart to see them die.

So she released sap. Sending it to them in a rush of sorrowful love for all the shade they'd given her, the flowers that scented her nights and the fruits that graced her mornings. The grien left her in powerful gush, a blessed release from pressure, one that ached with pleasurable pain, much like voiding a much-too-full bladder.

Naked branches tossed in a wind he couldn't feel, brown leaves and dried petals spiraling in tornadic frenzy, skittering up into the brilliant blue sky. A groaning, creaking sound muttered over the terrace. With a series of sharp booms, the stone planters burst, one after another, exploding rock shrapnel everywhere.

Behind her, Lonen laughed like a crazy man, exultant and wild, his excited energy shoring her up, like the sun at her back, Chuffta's steady presence in her mind a cool white counterpoint. Roots burst out of the planters, twining, lashing for purchase. The trunks thickened, writhing as they did, then shooting up, branches proliferating and leaves bursting into green vivid life. Blossoms followed, an induced spring racing faster than Grienon through the sky, followed by full summer, fruits burgeoning, weighing the branches even as they continued to thicken.

At this rate, they'd collapse. Or tear down her tower and them with it.

"It's too much!" she shrieked, suddenly panicked, which only made a shower of vines burst into radiant blossom.

"Then pull it back in. You know how." Chuffta's calm and rational mind-voice steadied her.

At the same time, something pinged against her mask. Lonen, tapping her metal cheek. "Enough, Oria," he said with implacable firmness. "Knock it back." His presence stabilized her, too, with his granite bedrock beneath the sunshine of his vivid personality.

Like releasing a handful of petals to the wind, she let go, the sgath and grien that had somehow combined into one power condensing, drawing back, and settling like a gentle rain.

Lonen kissed his fingertips and pressed them to the mask, just over her mouth, his aura bright with emotions, both extravagant and affectionate.

"You're a hell of a woman, Oria. And you're going to be a sorceress beyond imagining. Now let's go make you queen."

~ 13 ~

IT WASN'T HOW she'd expected to face the council, to demand to be ratified as Queen of Bára with a Destrye warrior at her side and her hands tingling from unleashing grien magic that still rattled the leaves of her garden.

Of course, she wasn't at all sure what she *had* envisioned, except that her mother was supposed to have handled this, as it was her plan and she was the former queen. She was supposed to have mastered the skill of envisioning a result so that it would manifest as she chose. Oria hadn't indulged herself with many expectations, as they'd inevitably led to disappointment. Time enough to learn all of that, she'd thought, if she ever mastered *hwil*. She'd never imagined things would happen so fast, one upon the next.

Or that her personal scale of sorrows and successes would alter quite so dramatically.

The nine-person council—composed of two priests, two priestesses, four folcwitas, who managed all nonmagical aspects of running Bára, headed by Folcwita Lapo, and High Priestess Febe—all seemed to frown at her as one. Captain Ercole, representing the City Guard, stood to the side as a non-voting consultant only. Though as Oria understood it, the council didn't exactly vote so much as attempt to persuade the titular heads of the body, those being the senior folcwita and high priest or priestess, to then advise the king or queen. With the current balance, it seemed that Febe had placed herself in the role of royal by adding an extra temple representative.

"Princess Oria," Folcwita Lapo puffed with the suspicion of an embattled man, "this is most irregular. Why are you here, bringing that Destrye—"

"King Lonen," she corrected in a cool, cutting tone.

"Not my king," he snapped back.

"Your king, yes, and your conqueror. Or have you forgotten so soon?" Lonen's voice rumbled at his most intimidating. Even his energy seemed larger, filling the room. Did he do it consciously? Probably not. Or maybe he did, having learned rapidly from her. Regardless, he affected them all, magically gifted and not.

Folcwita Lapo rose and steepled his hands on the semi-circular stone table, inclining his head at Lonen. "The council apologizes for the misunderstanding, King of the Destrye, but the treaty you believed valid is not. As Bára has no one on the throne at present, we are not in a position to pass binding law on anything." Yellow frustration oozed from him in light wisps.

"Your laws are irrelevant to me," Lonen replied, "except as my wife and I determine to uphold them."

Lapo glanced at Febe, puzzled. "His wife?"

"Behold your new queen," Lonen overrode any other reply. "Queen Oria of Bára."

Lapo laughed, while Febe continued to be silent, her sgath drawn tightly about her. The other priests and priestesses held physically still, impassive in their *hwil*, but the three junior folcwitas fell to whispering among themselves, one opening a tome of Báran law.

"The council has not ratified—"

"The council has no power to ratify anything without a royal on the throne of Bára," Oria cut in again. "You said as much yourself, Folcwita Lapo. I'm sure my father would express his gratitude to you, if he could, for holding this council and city together in this state of emergency. The burden has no doubt been great. However, I'm now ready to relieve you and High Priestess Febe of the mantle that should never have fallen upon you so heavily. I'm here to rule Bára as queen, as I was born to do and as my power and marriage entitles me to. Of course, I hope to retain all of you, for your good counsel for the benefit of all Bárans—less one priestess, naturally. It appears some imbalance has been introduced."

"Princess Oria," Febe said, not standing or moving at all, a statue of a priestess. "We all understand the strain that—"

"Queen or Your Highness," Oria stated. "You will address me properly."

Folcwita Lapo looked between them, then bent to speak into the ear of the folcwita with the law book.

"You are not queen until the temple crowns you as such." Febe's voice oozed with warning.

Oria waved a negligent hand. "Exactly. Which is why we are here. Truly I didn't expect you all to be so obtuse. My father, King Tavlor, always spoke so highly of this council's wisdom."

"The temple cannot seal the throne to—"

Folcwita Lapo held up a hand, tapping the law book. "No disrespect, High Priestess, but the law is very specific. In the absence of any of the royal family on the throne, when the first masked progeny of the previous ruler is married and presents themselves to the council, the temple is required to crown them as ruler of Bára. If Prin—Queen Oria has indeed been married by the temple, then all is in order."

"It's not an ideal marriage," Febe gritted out. "Not temple-blessed. He's a Destrye!"

"Were His Highness King Lonen and Her Highness Queen Oria duly married by the temple?" inquired the folcwita with the book, seemingly unaware that he pedantically repeated information already on the table.

"Yes," Febe conceded with ill grace, "by Priest Vico and myself, yesterevening, but they are obviously not an ideal match. His Highness is mind-dead. Her magic will go nowhere, possibly even turn back on itself."

Folcwita Lapo stewed with excitement. Febe had been injudicious, perhaps, in trying to overbalance the council in the temple's favor. It seemed she might have an unexpected ally in this. "Magic is the province of the temple," he said, bowing in Febe's direction. "As the keepers of Báran law, we note that the law books do not specify the magical quality of the marriage, only that there be one. Captain Ercole—what does the City Guard advise?"

"The guard stands with the law and the royal family," Captain Ercole replied, a solid, steady presence. "We support Queen Oria, naturally, as we supported her father and mother before her. The people will rejoice to have order restored after so long, and so much out of balance."

"Queen Oria." Febe kept her voice even, but her *hwil* cracked here and there. "Surely Your Highness does not wish to be Queen of Bára when your destiny lies with your new husband in Dru. We understand His Highness wishes to leave immediately for his homeland. We would not wish to delay you, King Lonen."

"I've changed my mind." Lonen sounded almost lazy, brushing a hand over Oria's braids, making one of the priestesses come alert with surprise beneath her *hwil*. In his determination to make a powerful show, he forgot to restrain himself and burned brightly with lust. But either she was becoming accustomed to his energy infiltrating hers, or because she'd burned off enough sgath, she absorbed it with relative ease. Even Folcwita Lapo's brash presence, which had buffeted her severely in the past, seemed little more than an uncomfortably hot breeze.

"I've come to like Bára," Lonen continued. "After all, it is mine, along with everything—and everyone—in it. Why not take my leisure to enjoy all my city has to offer?"

"You cannot be King of Bára, Your Highness," Febe said with considerable strain. "Only someone who's taken the mask can rule our city, by sacred law. You can only be the queen's consort."

The folcwita with the law book nodded, glancing up with an apologetic mien. Their excitement still hummed with bright hope, though Folcwita Lapo bowed to Lonen, showing his concern. "No dishonor to Your Highness, King Lonen."

"I am not concerned with such details," Lonen replied, attention on Oria and the braid he fingered. It was for show this time, however, not sending those waves of potent lust into her. Thankfully. "I have my kingdom, and yours. Oria can be Queen of Bára and I shall rule her. All the same in the end."

Insufferable oaf. He'd better have said that for show or they'd have words about it.

Febe rose slowly to her feet now. "Queen Oria, I beg of you. Bára begs you. You may not realize it, but your honored brother Prince Yar seeks an ideal bride. He'll return to Bára at any moment with her and they can rule as Sgatha and Grienon intend, as an ideal partnership, in a temple-blessed marriage. Bára needs this. You know it in your heart. Don't allow the Destrye this final victory over us. Our throne, the very bedrock of our lives, will be forever tainted."

Oria very nearly felt bad for the older woman. She truly believed in what she said, and had served Bára and the temple all her life. But she'd also been in favor of calling in the Trom, risking disaster with her remorseless drive to preserve those beliefs at all costs.

In the end life was more precious than any belief.

"Yes. You've grown wise, Oria."

"I try. Soon I'll be lecturing you."

Chuffta laughed, sending affection through her.

"Yar is not here and I am," she answered, speaking to them all. "For all we know he may not return with an ideal bride, who would still be foreign to Bára regardless. He might not return at all, as so many have not. My father would expect me to shoulder my ancient responsibility. My mother does expect it."

"The former queen is not here to support your claim," Febe protested. "You put words in her mouth."

"Are you calling me a liar, High Priestess?" Oria held onto her grien, but allowed her sgath to slide up against Febe's. "As your queen, I take exception to your tone. Perhaps the temple is in need of new leadership."

"You can't do that." The woman's *hwil* cracked a bit more, enough so one of the priests took note, moving in his chair. "You are not queen until I crown you."

"Then you had best crown me, or I'll put someone in charge who will."

Febe looked to Folcwita Lapo who radiated smug satisfaction at this point. He held up his palms. "Temple business falls to the temple and the royal family, as has been pointed out to the folcwitas many times. We keep secular law and all is in order. The folcwitas, the city guard, and—I feel confident in presuming to say—the people of Bára acknowledge Rhianna and Tavlor's daughter as queen. I see no reason for the temple to delay the final ritual."

Stiff necked, Febe inclined her head to Oria. "Very well. Though, as High Priestess, keeper of the sacred magics of Bára, I express grave reservations. Mark my words. This will be the day our revered city truly falls to the Destrye. You all seal our doom."

~ 14 ~

ONCE AGAIN, LONEN followed Oria through the palace halls to the temple. The Bárans, with their convoluted, even circular, laws and elaborate posturing sure came up short on preparations for rituals. No pomp and ceremony for this coronation.

Though he supposed he and Oria had that in common, as he'd taken his own father's wreath and sword on the battle-field. They'd never celebrated his ascent to the throne either, with so much work to do back in Dru. In truth, celebrating had been the last thing on his mind.

Still, hopefully that would change. He and Oria would not have to forever labor under the sawing need to address one crisis after the next. One day they would be in a better place, with their peoples fed and stable. With the gifts Oria had demonstrated on the rooftop, she could grow the crops the Destrye needed for several winters in the course of an afternoon. The impossible could be made possible indeed.

He eyed her slim, straight back as she preceded him, head held regally high. She'd looked incredible in the throes of working her magic. She'd nearly glowed with it, the force palpably sizzling against that internal part of him so sensitized to her. Other parts, too. He still throbbed with the arousal she'd incited. And from the vicious triumph that he'd not only

163

found a way to save the Destrye from the Trom, but in the same victory acquired a sorceress to feed them and a wife for himself replete with magical beauty. Had he been able, he would have seized her in a crushing kiss, barely leashing himself to only press one to her mask.

If they didn't find a way for him to bury his cock in her, he might lose his mind. Oh right—he'd already done that. Perhaps madness occurred in stages, growing ever worse. Cheerful thought.

Oria canted her head slightly in his direction, giving him the distinct impression of reproof. If he didn't need to help her keep it together through whatever Arill-cursed trial her people intended, he would have shared some of those salacious images. As it was, he would come up with a reasonable plan to give her pleasure as it was his duty to Arill to provide his wife. For himself, he might be thrown back to bitter youth, taking himself in hand several times a day while fantasizing about the woman he couldn't touch.

Probably a deserved fate, though that didn't mean he wouldn't fight it with every trick he possessed. He'd gotten very good at fighting.

High Priestess Febe paused at the bridge to the temple, stone-stiff in every line of her body. "Only the masked may enter the temple," she intoned, in what he'd come to think of as her priestess voice. It always seemed to bode ill. "King Lonen, you must remain without."

"Not happening," he replied in a level tone and taking Oria's sleeve, keeping her from leaving him. "I entered the temple before."

"For your wedding. The unmasked may enter at five times in their lives, the wedding is one."

He was not letting Oria face this alone. He'd much prefer,

in fact, if Oria had appointed a new temple head to perform the coronation ceremony. It seemed to be a foolish risk to have this woman, who so clearly resented and feared the prospect of Oria as queen, to have any power over her. She knew Oria's particular fragility and how to capitalize on it. What would stop her from gaming the ritual against Oria? From Oria's shoulder, Chuffta's eyes gleamed green and knowing. Could her Familiar read his thoughts, too? Regardless, it seemed they understood one another.

"What are the other occasions?" he inquired of the high priestess.

"The temple secrets are not yours to—"

"These are not temple secrets, High Priestess," Oria cut the woman off with that regal poise she'd put on as easily as she'd donned her mask. "This is something any Báran child knows. I apologize for our priestess, Your Highness. She is clearly overwrought and forgetting herself. The occasions are five, as on the fingers of a hand. The temple receives any and all at birth, byrebod, monahalgian, marriage, and death. Those with magical ability also may enter certain areas for instruction."

"What are byrebod and monahalgian?"

"Apologies, Your Highness—they are old terms, with no trade tongue correlations. They mean essentially presentation as an adult and consecration to the moons, respectively."

"I'm pledged to Arill, so there will be no consecration to the moons for me. What's involved in the other?"

Febe's featureless mask, for all the world seemed to smirk at him. "For men, it involves a ritual where he proves his manhood by demonstrating his fortitude, and by sealing a covenant."

That didn't sound bad, but Oria murmured, "Monahalgian would be easier on you. Surely your goddess will not mind a small transgression."

"I am loyal to all of my women, wives and goddesses," he muttered back. "Presentation as an adult for me, then I remain for the coronation."

"This is most irregular," Febe protested. "Are we to become a people who follow only the letter of the law and not the spirit of it under your reign, Queen Oria?"

Oria didn't exactly flinch, but the accusation clearly hit home—something he felt in his own gut—so he spoke up before she could waver.

"As Bára is mine, so am I hers. It's fitting that I present myself to the temple as every boy of the city does upon reaching his manhood. I consider this a covenant with Bára, which should be sufficient spirit to satisfy anyone."

Oria moved ever so slightly closer to him, relaxing the tautness of the silk sleeve he gripped, conveying her appreciation with the subtle gesture. Crazy how happy it made him that he'd pleased her. Though making her happy meant better fortune for the Destrye. He'd just think of it that way.

"Your Highness." Priest Vico stepped up. "While I'm delighted to perform your byrebod, particularly given the reasons you state, you should be aware that, ah, blood must be drawn." He tilted the mask significantly. "To seal the covenant," he added, not at all elucidating. "As a, uh, man."

"All right," Lonen replied slowly. The Bárans seemed to love drawing blood for their little rituals. The priest seemed to be waiting still, and it dawned on him. "Draw the blood from where?"

"Your … manhood," the priest answered in a much lowered voice, as if that added delicacy to it.

Lonen found himself gaping, then looked to Oria. "You went through this?"

"Women produce their own blood, don't they?" She said in a tart voice, clearly discomfited. "You needn't do this, Your Highness. Take your leisure and await me."

Barbarians, the lot of them. But Arill knew he'd shed plenty of blood. He'd just hoped never to be wounded there. Still, if the Báran boys could withstand it, a full Destrye warrior certainly could. Besides, he'd already made a pretty speech about it and couldn't very well back pedal on that. "We'll proceed as I outlined. Priest Vico will do my byrebod ceremony, followed by the coronation."

Priest Vico bowed. "As you will. Follow me, Your Highness."

"Queen Oria will come with me." The High Priestess turned to lead her away.

"No. The queen doesn't leave my sight," Lonen declared, letting himself growl over it, venting some of the aggravation over his impending ordeal. "She belongs to me and by my side she stays."

Priest Vico coughed and the high priestess went rigid. "Women do not attend a boy's byrebod," she declared.

"Or vice-versa," Vico added, not at all helpfully.

"I would assume that a boy has his byrebod well before he's married, yes?" At the priest's nod, Lonen continued. "A wife knows everything about her husband and her magic belongs to him, along with the succor of her body. Of course she would attend this important ceremony, should they occur in the reverse order."

"Most logical," Oria agreed.

Stymied, Febe bowed—stiffly, of course—and glided away. "I will await you in the ceremonial hall then, Your Highnesses."

Priest Vico gestured them to follow, but Lonen tugged

Oria's sleeve so she'd hang back.

"They don't cut off any important bits, do they?" he whispered to her.

"I wouldn't know, would I?" she hissed back. "As I'm not a *boy*."

"I can't believe your brothers wouldn't have hinted."

"Unlike you," she replied in a prim tone, lifting her chin, "they did not discuss their male parts with all and sundry."

"I don't discuss my cock with all and sundry—just with you, especially as you're so interested in it."

Her gasp of outrage took the edge off his nerves—and hers, he hoped—Chuffta's eyes glittering at him with what had to be amusement. The priest led him into a small chapel room, similar to the one they'd been married in the evening before. This one, however, looked entirely dedicated to Grienon, with representations of the small, dynamic moon in all his phases.

Priest Vico cleared his throat. "Normally, Your Highness, a boy is accompanied by his father, who has explained the ritual in advance. Or, failing that, another male relative."

"Just tell me what to do, man," Lonen answered. "Let's get it over with so we can move on."

"All right." He cleared his throat again. "Perhaps Queen Oria might wish to turn away and cover her ears?"

"Oh, for Sgatha's sake," she snapped, "I can muffle my eyes and ears and sgath will still show me—" She broke off abruptly, her mask swiveling to the sky beyond the stone temple ceiling. "No," she whispered, putting a hand to Chuffta's tail wrapped around her wrist.

"What?" Lonen asked. Then grabbed her sleeve when she only shook her head. "What is it?"

A sound broke through his words. He knew that sound, like the dull roar of a bonfire. The giant fire-breathing draconic cousins to the derkesthai, mounts of the Trom.

"Too late," Oria said, her voice hard, echoing against the metal mask.

He wasn't sure if she meant for him, or for them all.

~ 15 ~

"MAYBE THAT'S A riderless dragon roaring. Or could it be Yar returning?" Lonen asked her, unstrapping the battle axe from his back.

"I don't think it's either." She didn't sense Yar anywhere near the city. But that densely powerful black sun her sgath revealed was familiar. She hadn't been skilled enough before to get so much detail about their magical signature, but she recognized them just the same. "Yar may be behind this, however. They have not returned since you left, but I think the Trom are here now."

"They are here, yes." Chuffta's mind voice shivered with trepidation. Very little frightened the derkesthai, but his larger cousins certainly seemed to.

"The High Priestess," Priest Vico said, fear leaking through the *hwil*. "Febe would have summoned them, rather than give you the crown."

Oria stared at him in stunned surprise. "She is the summoner?"

His mask bobbed. "She and Yar both, as priest and priestess. I, myself, do not possess enough grien for the task She worked with him to do it."

"You could have warned me." Anger burned in her. Along with the terror. The feeling of that thing touching her. Those matte black eyes staring into her heart and finding a mirroring darkness. *Princess Ponen.*

"I wanted to, but we were sworn to tell only the king or queen. Since you're effectively queen now…" he trailed off, voice weakening.

Wonderful. Oria spun to the doors, hissing when Lonen brushed the skin of her hand before he clamped his own on her forearm over her sleeve. "Sorry for that. Clumsy of me, but you're not racing out there."

She struggled back the near overwhelming surge of his emotional energy that the brief touch sent rocketing through her nervous system. An intense stew of terror, love, battle rage, despair, determination, hope, and more than she could sort even with the luxury of hours, not moments.

"What choice do I have?" She tried to pull away, but he held on, his touch burning through the layers of silk. "You're hurting me."

He let go, but moved his big body between her and the doorway. "I'm not letting you confront those creatures."

"You know what they'll do! You've seen it with your own eyes. I can't let them kill my people just to get to me." All those piles of lifeless flesh… she couldn't bear for it to happen again.

"How do you know they won't kill you too?" Lonen shimmered large in her sgath, full of furious frustration.

"They won't. Or can't. You saw that too. I'm something to them. I don't know what, but they won't kill me. I have to confront them."

He seethed with conflict, the image slamming into her of him picking her up and carrying her off to some safe bower. "If you're going, I go with you."

"Lonen—they *can* kill *you.* Don't make me stand by while

you're turned nothing but boneless heap before my eyes."

"I won't attack. They don't kill if we show no aggression."

"You can't be sure of that."

"Just as you can't be sure that they won't kill you this time."

Stymied, she fumed at him. "Please stay here. I'm asking this of you."

"No. I said that you don't leave my side and I meant it." He touched her masked cheek and managed a lopsided smile. "At least this keeps the priest's knife away from my jewels a little longer."

She shook her head, amazed he'd made her laugh under such dire circumstances. "I can't believe you were going to let him do that in the first place."

"Nothing gets between me and a goal. I told you that."

Yes, he had. And what Lonen said, he meant—and made happen. She could use that.

"Then remember this," she said, leaning as close to him as she dared, keeping his full attention. "You've said over and over that you're going to find a way to bed me."

Desire rode high in his gamut of emotional energy, though he responded evenly enough. "What are you getting at?"

"You'd better keep that in mind, because that's a goal and if you let the Trom kill you, it'll never happen. Think on that."

His stunned and grudgingly admiring amusement did a great deal to take the edge off her nerves. She began to understand why he enjoyed teasing her. He kept himself in front of her as she walked, a pace ahead with his signature big, bold strides as they hurried out the front doors of the temple. He carried his battle-axe two-handed, a black hole of a barrier before her.

"Leave the axe behind," she urged.

He didn't hitch even momentarily, but his incredulity swamped her. "Not even if Arill Herself asked me."

She had to run to do it—Chuffta half spreading his wings to keep balance on her shoulder—but she managed to draw level with him, grabbing onto his leather-clad arm, glad of his thicker Destrye clothes that buffered some of the impact from her impetuous move. He glanced down at her in some surprise, all of him softening, and he slowed somewhat. "Don't fret. I learned my lesson, too. As long as I'm not aggressive towards it, I should be fine."

"Last time you insisted that *I* put down *my* sword!"

"Because you could hardly lift the cursed thing," he retorted grimly. "I don't know what in Arill you were thinking. If we survive all this, I'm going to teach you to use a weapon your own size."

"I don't need a weapon. I'm a sorceress. Magic is all I need."

"Then this would be an excellent time to use it." He came to a halt, swiftly sheathing his axe on his back. Not one, but three Trom stood at the bridge to the temple. The sight of them turned her stomach, their magic like Chuffta's, but as much greater in intensity as the dragons were to him in size, nearly blinding her sgath with the radiance of it.

She'd been too mind-blind to see it before, their charismatic immensity. To the physical eye, they looked like desiccated husks of humans, skin as dry as old leaves stretched over bones, like corpses left to dry in the desert. As if to make up for all they lacked in robust humanity, concentrated magic filled them out on the non-physical plane. It extended inward also, each of them seeming to carry a black star of contained power and paradoxically infinite magic.

It made them hard to look at, the way their magic moved

both out and in, as if they existed in multiple places at once, giving her a vague sense of nausea and dislocation.

"I did not see it before, either, but I do through you now. Most … disconcerting."

"What does it mean?"

"Nothing good."

"Steady, Oria," Lonen said as she swayed on her feet, briefly cupping the back of her head over her braids. A fleeting touch that nevertheless heartened her. "I'm taking cues from you now."

Of course he handed her the decision-making power when she had no idea what to do. The Trom saved her from deciding, however.

"Queen Ponen," the one in front greeted her with its mouthless voice that emanated from its entire being. "It gladdens us to see you've taken not one, but several steps farther down your path."

She hated to contemplate what that might mean. "Bára greets you. We did not expect you to return."

The Trom couldn't smile, of course, and yet it seemed to. Much in the same way that expressions sometimes conveyed themselves from the masked priests and priestesses. She suppressed a shudder and Lonen shifted towards her, his desire to wrap her in his arms palpable. It helped, oddly enough.

"We come when summoned. Though it's true it was not your call we answered. Someday you will call to us and your understanding will deepen."

No doubt that day would come—had to, if she planned to wrest control of them from Yar and Febe—but she dreaded discovering what that deeper understanding boded for her. No sign of either of those summoners, cowards that they were, so she took the situation in hand. "None stands here who summoned you, so you may leave again."

They didn't move. "You do not yet command our obedience," the leader replied, just as it had when they met before. If it was, indeed, the same being. Difficult to discern.

Silence whistled through the chasm, a hot wind kicking up a swirl of sand on stone. Lonen's desperate curiosity to know what the Trom said reminded her that they spoke a language he didn't know but she somehow understood.

"*Mind to mind,*" Chuffta said.

Ah, yes.

"We will see the one who summoned us, as required." The Trom spoke as if observing the weather, without inflection.

Much as she disliked Febe, Oria couldn't stomach watching her turned to pulp by the Trom, nor did she wish to hand power to the High Priestess in case the dread guardians would respond to her commands.

"The priest you seek is not within the city," she replied, willing the honesty of that to suffice to convince them to leave.

"But I am." Febe stepped before them, her sgath shivering with her temerity, her *hwil* strained. Both afraid and tremulously delighted with herself. "As Summoner, I invite you to enter the temple."

Lonen swore at that, able to understand those ritual words from the previous ceremonies, though he did not draw his axe, his hands clenching into fists and rage going black. "Stay behind me, Oria."

And watch him die? Never. She didn't move, staying right beside him as the three Trom crossed. "Summoner," the lead Trom greeted the high priestess. "What do you require of us?"

"Kill this one." Febe pointed at Oria.

~ 16 ~

EVERYTHING BLURRED INTO a high, colorless whine in his head. Even as Lonen reached for his axe determined to die protecting Oria if he had to, Chuffta spread his wings, breathing green fire that raised the already broiling temperature on the exposed bridge to unbearable levels. Oria's magic, too, as familiar on his skin now as her scent in his head, billowed up. Tornadic gusts spun into life, catching Chuffta's fire into swirls.

The Trom remained untouched by any of it, as if encased in one of Oria's transparent drinking glasses. The leader regarded Oria and Chuffta, then stepped closer without concern for the fire, unbuffeted by the wind and sand that scoured Lonen's exposed skin. Axe in hand, he moved to intercept the thing's lethal caress.

And found himself immobilized. By Oria's magic, Arill take her.

"Oria!" he shouted, fighting her grip that held him as surely as chains. "Release me, curse you."

She shouted an unintelligible reply, her voice harsh as a carrion bird's.

The Trom spoke, strange words he couldn't parse. But Chuffta stopped the defensive fire and Oria lowered her hands, seeming stunned. Whatever it said, Febe understood and clenched her fists in impotent rage.

"If you won't kill her, then kill him," she screeched over the howling wind.

"No!" To his terror, Oria imposed her slim form between his frozen one and the Trom.

"Defend him and die at their touch," Febe crowed her victory. "Lose him and join your broken mother as a widow who will never gain the crown."

Oria raised her hands. "I'll take option number three." As it had on the rooftop, her powerful grien magic surged, gaining that sharp edge, and struck the high priestess like a giant fist.

She staggered. "Impossible!" the woman nearly howled. "Abomination! You'll die for this. Kill her. Protect me and kill the foul grien user."

"Not me, not today," Oria said, quietly enough that he almost didn't hear it. Abruptly her magic released him as she drew it back, her braids snapping in the unfelt wind of it.

With a cry of despair, Febe fell, punched again by the fist, then scrabbled for purchase, fingers sliding on the sand as an invisible grip dragged her to the edge of the chasm.

"Mercy, I beg you!" she sobbed.

Then Febe plummeted over the edge, her long, wailing cry echoing back before attenuating into nothing.

Brutally reminded of his brother's death by the same unending fall, horror crawled through Lonen's heart. But he still had Oria to defend. She recklessly still stood between him and the Trom.

"The Summoner is dead," she declared, her voice reverberating with strange harmonies. "You may depart."

All three inclined their heads to her and the first spoke. They turned and walked over the bridge, disappearing back into the palace. Moments later, three dragons lifted into the sky and wheeled out of sight.

Suddenly realizing by the scream of his straining shoulders that he still held the axe mid-swing, Lonen lowered it, then spoke to Oria's back. "If you ever do anything like that again, I'll kill you myself."

ORIA, UNBELIEVABLY EXHAUSTED, could barely keep to her feet. Not in the overloaded, close to breaking sense, but in a different way, one she'd never experienced before. Her mask moved slickly over her sweating face and she longed to be rid of the thing—especially as her sgath showed the world only dimly, as if through a haze of smoke. Empty and aching, she turned to face Lonen.

"I could say the same back to you."

"It's not funny." He sounded weary, too.

"I didn't mean it as a joke. But it's irrelevant now. They're gone." *For now*, she didn't say, though the unspoken words hung in the air between them.

Lonen acknowledged that with a grunt. "Are you all right?"

"Yes." Though she wasn't sure of the truth of that. She felt… odd. But physically unharmed.

"What did they say to you—why didn't it kill you when Febe commanded it?"

"I—" She didn't want to give voice to it any more than she already had. That the Trom had told Febe they could no more kill her than one of their own. And it wasn't clear if they'd meant they actually couldn't or if they didn't want to. "I'll tell you about it later. We must go through with the coronation."

"You're clearly exhausted," he said in a neutral enough tone, though his concern and frustration with her snapped and snarled like two dogs fighting over the last piece of meat. "You have to rest and build up your reserves, or you might not survive whatever the ritual involves."

"We don't have time." It ticked away inside her, the imminence of Yar's return.

"That's not the most important consideration at this point," he insisted.

"You were the one who came to me for help." She would have snapped it, but she didn't have the energy. Really she wanted to sit. If she could just sit on the ground for a moment or two. Or lie down…

Lonen snapped fingers in front of her mask. "You're dead on your feet. Let's go back to your tower."

"I can't help you if I don't have control of the Trom, and I can't do that unless I'm queen. We're so close—let's just go in the temple and get it over with."

"Oria." Lonen spoke her name sternly enough to command her attention, if not her obedience. "Arill knows I was willing to let that priest near my cock with a knife so you could get that crown on your head, or whatever you Bárans do, but you won't be any good to Dru or Bára if you're dead. I am not letting you do this right now."

"You don't get to boss me around, Destrye."

"He has a good point, Oria—you're very tired and you have very little sgath in you."

"It's not fair," she complained to both of them, vaguely aware that she sounded pitiful and whiny. "Either I have too much energy in me or not enough. I'm sick to death of being fragile."

Lonen laughed. "Right—so damn fragile that you knocked

that priestess into the chasm like a woman sweeping dirt off the porch."

She choked back the remorse. Febe had tried to kill her, but Oria had never thought she'd be capable of murder. Though once the priestess had realized the truth about Oria's grien magic… Well, there had been no choice.

"Come on." Lonen said more gently. "Let me be strong for you. I can carry you up, if you'll let me."

"It's too far," she protested. "Even you can't climb all those stairs carrying me."

"How do you think you got up there last night?" A few mischievous sparks made it through to her weakened sgath vision. "Besides, you weigh no more than a kitten."

"A kitten!" She sputtered, unable to come up with a retort.

"A drowned kitten." He leaned in, wrapping her in his bracing energy, for once only a comfort and not at all too much to bear. "All fur and spitting feistiness."

"You did *not* just call me feisty." She thought that had put up her back enough to rally, but she swayed on her feet.

"Better to retreat and rest to fight tomorrow, than to surely suffer defeat today."

"And if Yar arrives?"

She'd asked Chuffta, but Lonen replied. "Then we cut down that tree when we come to it. Let me carry you, Oria." He pulled his mantle off his shoulders, setting it around her, then strapped his axe again to his back. "That will be hot, but will protect you from my touch. Say yes."

"Fine," she replied, if only because she'd run out of energy to argue. Maybe even to stand, the way she swayed on her feet. "With the sun going down, I'm a little chilled anyway."

"Only a Báran could say such a thing. Chuffta, man, do a buddy a favor and either fly or ride on my shoulder."

"He says he'll fly so he won't score your flesh, but that if you get padding, he'd ride your shoulder in the future." She drew the cloak around her, making sure it covered her skin. "I'm ready."

She braced herself for the searing contact, but he slipped gentle arms familiarly beneath her shoulders and knees, easily lifting and tucking her against his muscled chest. With easy strides, he crossed the bridge and carried her through the palace.

Dreamily, she let her sgath vision go, closed her physical eyes, too, and simply absorbed the scent and feel of him. So familiar already. "This is so easy for you," she remarked.

"I'm getting quite a lot of practice," he replied in that wry tone of his.

She winced, opened her mouth to apologize, remembered she shouldn't, and sighed instead. "I wish I wasn't like this."

"I understand why you say that, but don't. Your blessing and your curse. Without this, you can't have the other—and your sorcery is fantastic to behold. I wouldn't change a thing about you." To her surprise, he pressed a kiss to her mask over her forehead, his energy swirling with a tenderness that disarmed her. "Well, maybe I'd change that stubborn temper of yours. And your reckless bravery."

"And the fact that you can't bed me," she reminded him.

"Oh, I'll find a way to bed you, Oria. Mark my words on that. You promised me if I survived the Trom, that would happen."

"I'm sure I never said such a thing." She yawned.

"That's how I heard it." He sounded insufferably pleased with himself.

"And you call me stubborn. You're worse."

"Oh yes, my lovely sorceress. More stubborn than you are

by a far stretch, so you might as well give up and succumb to my manly charms."

They were just passing through the main doors of the palace, about to take the turn to her tower when he halted. Then cursed, using Arill's name.

"What?" She reached to see with sgath. Like lighting a too-short candle wick, it sputtered, then died, leaving her effectively blind. She reached for the magic below Bára, but it trickled in far too slowly to replenish her stores anytime soon. Much as she hated to acknowledge it, Lonen had been correct about not facing the coronation ceremony.

"Oria—there's an entourage at the bridge to Ing's Chasm. I think it's—"

"I think Yar has returned," Lonen spoke at the same time.

~ 17 ~

"**P**UT ME DOWN," Oria commanded. Because she sounded more like her imperious self and not the bone-weary waif of before, he acceded. But he kept a hand near the small of her back, in case she fainted.

"I'm not going to faint," she said irritably, making him smile.

"At least you're feeling spry enough to read my mind again. I've been thinking all sorts of things that you missed."

"Perhaps I chose not to sully my own mind by looking," she replied in that lofty, prim tone. If her odious brother hadn't been crossing the bridge to the palace, he'd have sent her an image to make her lose that composure. Chuffta winged in, angling through the open palace doors to accommodate his wide wingspan, sinuous neck snaked back in flight like the great fishing birds that frequented the lakes of Dru. Oria held up her left forearm and he landed there as neatly as any tamed raptor might.

The three of them waited in resigned silence, with increasing resignation, as it became clear that the young prince had indeed brought a priestess with him. The pair led a joyful procession up from the gates below, both in their golden masks, though hers was of a slightly different style, and she wore yellow silk robes instead of crimson. They walked arm in arm, sleeves drawn back and her forearm laid over his, their hands laced together. A posture even Lonen recognized as a blatant display of their compatibility. He'd never thought to experience a jagged bolt of envy for another man's fortune with a woman, but he hated that Yar and his future bride already enjoyed what remained a distant promise for him and Oria.

Unfair to them both, but Arill bestowed Her blessings according to wisdom known only to Her.

"Steady, Destrye," Oria murmured, her usual epithet sounding more like an endearment. Was she even aware of the shift? For a moment she leaned into his hand resting lightly on the cloak covering her. A gesture as potent as the most intimate caress.

Yar caught sight of them, hitched, then strode forward at an increased pace, his priestess fiancée losing some of her grace as she hustled not to be dragged along by the impetuous boy. "Oria," he called. "What is the meaning of this? Why is this bar—"

"Prince Yar," she cut him off, "allow me to present my husband, King Lonen of the Destrye."

All fell silent. Captain Ercole hastened up. "Forgive me, Queen Oria, I would have sent word, but you were in the temple."

"No apologies needed, Captain, I—"

"*Queen?*" Yar's voice rose perilously, the priestess still on his arm flinching away ever so slightly. She wore her very blond hair in two big plaits that wrapped up to form a sort of crown. "You cannot be queen—I am King of Bára now!"

"I married in Bára's temple first," she replied implacably. "I greet you, my future sister."

"Greetings, future sister, Queen Oria" the priestess inclined her head. "Thank you for—"

"Don't call her that," Yar strangled over the words. Lonen imagined the prince's face going red and purple with impotent rage. "It can't be a temple-blessed marriage. Not married to that barbarian, mind-dead Destrye."

"Yar!" Oria's tone was cutting. "You are being unforgivably rude to your brother, His Highness King Lonen."

"No insult taken," Lonen replied, giving them all the lazy smile—and attendant image—of the forest cat cleaning its claws. "I am at peace with being both mind-dead and Destrye, though it seems others than myself demonstrate barbaric behavior. Greetings, future sister. Are you gifted with a name?"

"I am Gallia of Lousá. Greetings Your Highness."

"My marriage trumps yours," Yar spoke over his bride-to-be with newfound confidence, earning a twitch of annoyance from Gallia. "Especially as you clearly have not yet been crowned. Sloppy of you, dear sister. Otherwise you might have won the race. I admit you've surprised me with this … unorthodox move. But you've sacrificed your lifelong happiness along with any chance your progeny may have had to hold Bára for nothing. You married in the temple first, but High Priestess Febe will join us in a temple-blessed marriage for our ideal match."

"High Priestess Febe is dead, Prince Yar." Priest Vico stepped up with smooth manners, bowing as he delivered the news.

Yar paused, reassessing. "How is this possible?"

"The Trom killed her," Oria supplied, lying with admirable ease. "She summoned them and they killed her." She rubbed Chuffta between the eyes, appearing to be completely relaxed. Faking her *hwil* most likely. Then she lifted her mask to face Yar's. "At least we now know who the Summoner was, which means we shall not be disturbed by them again. I might rest easy, yielding the throne to you—perhaps even retiring with my husband to Dru—knowing that the Trom will never be called on, for any reason."

She layered meaning into her words, delivering both a promise and a subtle warning. No one there need know of Yar's culpability, if he agreed to suspend his attacks on the Destrye. Though Gallia remained still and apparently serene, Lonen thought she paid very close attention to the exchange. Yar covered his fiancée's hand with his, stroking her skin, clearly taunting Oria with the gesture.

"I don't need Febe. I have another priestess and her magic will be mine," he said with soft menace. "I shall call on whatever power I wish. For the good of Bára. Your loyalties are questionable, my sadly delicate sister. Perhaps your recent... difficulties have made you mentally unstable. There's precedent for that in the females of our family, as all have witnessed."

The folcwita from the council session who'd been the keeper of the law books cleared his throat. He spoke sofly to Priest Vico, who nodded with interest. "It seems," the priest said in a voice that carried through the hall, "that there is provision for equally qualified married couples to demonstrate their compatibility and abilities to the temple leadership, who then judge who will be crowned."

"Nonsense," Yar snarled, hand tightening on Gallia in a way that made Lonen twitch to stop him. "We will be king and queen. You'll marry us immediately."

"I will marry you now, yes, but tomorrow both couples will present themselves for my judgement. As is my sacred responsibility as High Priest of the temple of Bára."

"I'll replace you," Yar said.

"Only the king or queen can do that," Priest Vico replied implacably, "and neither you nor Princess Oria can claim that rank as yet."

"That solution is satisfactory to me," Oria inserted, sounding unconcerned, but the way she leaned into his supporting hand made her think she wearied. "King Lonen and I will meet you tomorrow. Congratulations on your wedding, to you both. I regret that we cannot attend the post-celebration."

"Prince Yar," Gallia spoke up. "As you know, the journey between cities strained me considerably. I'd prefer to—"

"What?" Yar cut her off. "You'd prefer to let my sister be crowned and leave you without the throne you left Lousá for? Your family and temple would be greatly displeased, especially to lose the many bride gifts I offered."

She inclined her head graciously. On Oria's arm, Chuffta ruffled his wings, the tip of his tail twitching where it dangled off her wrist, the only indication of her disquiet.

"Don't worry, my sweet." Yar gathered himself and stroked Gallia's hand, with a glee that was nevertheless avaricious. "It will require very little to demonstrate the superiority of our marriage. Look at them—she cannot even bear his touch skin-to-skin, much less give him any magic. We can win the throne, be crowned, and return to our wedding bed. I have heirs to beget."

"Of course," Gallia murmured.

"To the temple then," Priest Vico said, leading the way.

Oria wouldn't want to show weakness, so Lonen offered his sleeved arm to lean upon, glad that she took advantage of the support as he escorted her away from the less-than-joyful couple. Once her guard locked the doors to her tower behind them, she sagged and Chuffta took wing. Without asking, Lonen swept her up in his arms, and she sighed with relief, letting him carry her without protest.

~ 18 ~

S HE LIKED BEING in Lonen's arms, all safe and comfortable—which were not things she'd expected to ever feel with him. He ascended the stairs with tireless stamina, seeming as if he could carry her forever. Maybe he could.

"I never thought I'd feel sorry for an ideally matched couple," she finally said, after he'd climbed for some time. Without either her sgath or her physical sight, she couldn't be sure how far they'd come, but it felt like nearly halfway.

"I figured you for asleep."

"No—just thinking. All my life I wanted that, what Gallia has. It's what every girl dreams of. The perfect husband and an ideal marriage. All a lie."

"What Gallia has is a vicious idiot for a husband. I don't suppose you could have stopped it."

"Yar is young…" And she was running out of excuses for him. "But no. She would not have thanked me for intervening. Yar is correct that her family and temple would ostracize her for refusing an ideal match, especially one that will make her Queen of Bára. At least it seems as if she'll make a good queen, from the little I saw of her."

"You're so certain we'll lose tomorrow?"

"Of course we'll lose." He'd surprised her. Even in his eternal optimism, he had to recognize that they couldn't possibly triumph in a contest of that sort.

"Priest Vico favors you. If he can, he'll call it for you."

"*If* being the operative word. We'll likely have to demonstrate physical contact, as Yar and Gallia did so blatantly."

"Is that not usual?"

"Bárans are formal about physical contact in public, for obvious reasons. Yar's display wasn't quite obscene, but it was rude. Especially with a priestess new to our people. He did not accord her the respect he should have."

He made a mental note of that, to show Oria respect according to her customs, which were far more formal than those of the Destrye. "What else will the testing involve?"

"Almost certainly performing feats of magic. Meaning you would have to use grien, drawing on my sgath. Two impossible obstacles, right there—and don't take that as a challenge," she added emphatically, immediately regretting using that word at all.

"Too late." Lonen sounded far too cheerful. "You've set the stakes for me, my sorceress fair."

She groaned. "Lonen, we can't win this. We'll have to find another way to help the Destrye."

"Keep talking—every disclaimer makes me want to triumph that much more."

"Put me down. I can walk."

"Not so tired now?"

"I'm feeling more energized." Indeed, Lonen's bracing proximity refilled her empty spaces with surprising rapidity, her sgath vision returning with, if not its usual clarity, a very decent level considering she'd been cleaned out not long before.

"Excellent news," he said, not putting her down. "But save your strength. I have plans for it."

Her face went hot. "You can't be thinking that—"

To his credit, he waited for her to finish the sentence until it became clear she wouldn't. "Exactly."

"Lonen."

"Oria," he echoed in the same tone of exasperation.

She wouldn't reward his mischievous behavior by laughing.

"Look," he said. "Part of the deal tomorrow is demonstrating our compatibility and the solidity of our marriage, yes? How can we do that if *you* don't believe I can be a real husband to you?"

"I think I have very good reasons for my doubts," she said quietly, not wanting to dampen his spirits, but whatever he had in mind, he would come away disappointed.

"That's why I need to convince you." He pressed a kiss to her mask, as he had before, but pausing in his climb to let it linger. "Say you'll give me the chance to try."

"Will you encase me in metal then?" She meant to sound scathing, but it came out breathless. This close to him, the ardent energy of his desire flowed through her in inescapable waves.

"Something like that. Will you trust me?"

"I don't know."

He stopped entirely. "Yes or no. And before you answer, let me remind you of how much you've trusted me already. This is a small thing compared to your life."

"It doesn't feel like a small thing." Her heart thudded in dread. Or anticipation? So difficult to know.

"Are you afraid?"

"I'm not an idiot. Of course I'm afraid of that pain."

"Am I hurting you now?"

"Well, no, but—"

"I'm going to interrupt that 'but.' It will be pleasure only, Oria." He swarmed with earnest hope and desire, steely determination beneath. "Pleasure that Arill bestows upon us, so that people who love can share themselves intimately. Let me have that with you."

She couldn't resist him, and she suspected he knew it. "Fine." She blew out the capitulation on a long breath, and he resumed climbing with an increased, even jaunty stride. No telling what she'd just agreed to.

"I don't suppose Chuffta hunts at night?" he asked.

"I will give you privacy," her Familiar immediately chimed in. *"I will not be listening, so call loudly should you need me."*

She felt unexpectedly bereft. Chuffta hadn't been away from her thoughts since she was a child.

"I'm still only a loud thought away. And you're a woman grown. You deserve a little private joy."

"Thank you. I love you."

"And I love you." He withdrew from her, with one last affectionate and wordless thought.

"He's giving us privacy," she told Lonen.

"Good man. I wondered if your connection to him is part of why you never experimented with pleasuring yourself."

She had to keep from squirming, knowing he'd feel it. "I really don't want to discuss that."

"Oria, sweetheart—you just gave me permission to do a lot more than talk about sex with you. And we have a bit of a climb still. Help me understand you. Having sex with me will be a lot more intimate than talking about it."

She was afraid of that, which meant she might as well start conditioning herself to this exposure. Not unlike learning to be around people in the first place. "I'm sure that's part of it, but I also never really felt the urge."

"Never? Not even a little?" He sounded entirely dubious.

"No." Except those books. They'd made her feel this way, too, which was entirely wrong.

"Tell me what you're thinking," Lonen murmured.

"Are you certain you can't read my thoughts?" She could understand why it discomfited him that she could read his.

"Not exactly, but your body reveals a great deal—especially when I'm holding you like this."

"I really could walk."

"Not happening. I'm enjoying myself too much. What were you thinking?"

"Oh, it's wrong and awful and embarrassing. I can't say."

He was quiet a moment. "Does it have to do with how much it aroused you to talk about surrendering to me?"

If she hadn't been wearing her mask, she would have clapped her hands over her face. "Lonen…"

"You might as well tell me," he said, with those teasing sparks, but also with soothing images of cuddling her and keeping her safe. "You know I won't stop asking questions until I wear you down."

That was the truth. "I can't believe I'm going to tell you this."

"I can believe it. If nothing else, you at least trust me to take care of you."

Also true, rational or not. How it had happened that she trusted a Destrye warrior with her emotional well-being more than her mother or brother… Her world continued to alter, not content with upending, but also insisting on twisting sideways and in all sorts of unpredictable directions. Why not this aspect, too?

She took a steadying breath, reaching for *hwil*. "When I was young, I saw these illustrations in the history books."

"Yes?" he prompted when she faltered. "What of?"

"Of Destrye taking women captive, tied up with rope, and—ugh—I felt things then, which is horrible of me." She waited for his reproof, seething with humiliated shame, an echo of the priestess's scorn when she caught Oria rapt over those books, taking them away and advising her that meditation would do far more to build *hwil*.

"I thought as much." He said instead, full of male satisfaction.

"But I don't want that," she hastened to make sure he understood. "I don't know why it affected me. I don't want it to happen, I'm only saying that's the only time before that I felt any … urges."

"Before what?"

"Recently," she said, hoping to stop things there. No such luck, of course.

"Before meeting me?"

"Maybe," she muttered, but he only grew more pleased with himself.

"You get under my skin, too. For a long time I thought it was magic, that you'd somehow bewitched me."

She sat up a little straighter, indignant. "I would never!"

"Don't spit, kitten. I know that now. More important, I understand something of those desires you speak of and can give you a taste of them."

"If you try to rape me, I will use everything in me to kill you," she warned him, chill dread mixing with the heat of longing.

Absurdly, he laughed. "I have no doubt you could and would, my sorceress wife, with those weapons you wield so well. I promise you—no rape. No pain or fear. Only a glimpse to open that window, to allow you to feel what made those illustrations so compelling."

"I still don't understand how you can possibly do this without touching my skin," she muttered, rebellious and intrigued.

"I'm an inventive man when I want something."

~ 19 ~

GAINING THE TOP of the tower, he carried Oria straight to her bedroom. Their bedroom, he supposed. Far from feeling tired from the climb, his body surged with fevered excitement. Oria would be his at last. A wedding night to remember, if somewhat delayed. He set her on her feet where she remained, watching him light candles in the glass lanterns, suspicion in every line of her body.

"Lonen..." she started as he gently turned her by the shoulders, facing her away from him.

"I'm only removing your mask and taking down your hair," he soothed her.

She laughed, a little ragged. "I should have known that would be first."

"Indeed you should have," he agreed, working more quickly this time, having tied the knots himself. "Whenever we're alone, this will be first. Can we agree to that?"

"I suppose that's not too much to ask." She handed him the mask to set beside the bed, trading him for one of the cool cloths that Juli left for her in the covered jar. Oria used it to mop her face—and to keep it shielded, he suspected, as he took down her braids and brushed out the rippling copper mass of her hair.

"What are you thinking?" she whispered.

"Aren't you listening?"

"I'm trying not to do that as much."

"I don't mind," he told her, discovering to his surprise that he really didn't. "In fact, I'm finding I like having you in my head." He drew his hands through her hair, savoring the silky heft of it. "A way of being close to you, since I can't yet be inside your body."

She relaxed fractionally. "Then you won't…"

"Won't hurt you. I know what the limits are. Trust me."

Letting out a breath, she set the face cloth aside. "I do."

"Enough to take off your robes?"

She hesitated fractionally, then nodded, first untying his mantle and giving it back to him. Bemused, he tossed it aside, watching her. It would be so much easier if he could first kiss her, seduce her with gentle caresses. But she wasn't a woman to be cozened regardless. She had her own style of boldness, once she set herself on a course of action.

She blushed, eyes hooded, but unfastened the robes without faltering further, shedding the layers of them, until she stood only in that thin white chemise, in a pool of crimson silk. Still not looking at him, she pulled at the ties, then dropped the undergarment as well, standing naked before him.

Arill had blessed him with such a glorious woman. If She also gave him the challenge of being unable to touch his wife's skin, then he accepted that as the price.

Slim as a sapling, skin luminous in the candlelight with her radiant cape of metallic hair surrounding her, Oria took his breath away. Her breasts were tipped with small nipples, a rose as delicate as Sgatha's light, and the hair at her mons glinted a copper so smooth and straight he ached to taste her with his tongue.

Someday, they would find a way.

She studied his reaction, probably reading his emotions, so he let her feel it—the astounding desire and awe of her exotic beauty. Receiving the message, she smiled. Tentative, even shy at first, then blooming with all her radiance.

"I am relieved to be pleasing to you," she said quietly, surprising him.

"How could you have doubted it?"

Her shimmy of a shrug made her breasts bounce enticingly. Clearly Arill planned to test his restraint and self-control severely. He'd asked Her for a penance to cleanse his spirit of the taint of his deeds and She had delivered. Hopefully he'd emerge from it a better person, if somewhat crazed.

"I've never been naked for a man," Oria was saying, so he dragged his fascinated gaze up to her face. "And I know I am not at all like Nat—your Destrye women."

Because she'd seen Natly in his mind. Arill only knew what all she'd seen of Natly there.

"Nor am I like your Báran men," he returned, then caught himself, struck. She'd said he intimidated her with his size, and he was darker, hairier than any Báran he'd seen. "Do I revolt you?"

She gave him a curious smile. "Those illustrations, remember?"

How perfect that she'd shared that with him. It made many things easier, and he hoped to deliver on that long-held fantasy. "On that note, hold out your wrists, crossed in front of you." He picked up one of her many silk scarves and drew close enough to scent her heating skin.

She eyed him uncertainly, but those eyes also showed her arousal, her dark pupils wide. "We're really doing this?"

"It ups the tension, speaks to your fantasy—and mine, I might add—and has the bonus of keeping you still so I won't accidentally touch your skin with mine."

She took a deep breath and held out her crossed wrists, gaze on his face. Not the dying doe, life bleeding away at his hands, but an ardent woman trusting him to deliver on his promises. The absolution he'd looked for. Wrapping the silk in and around her wrists, tying the knots just so to keep her delicate bones from crushing together, he vowed to never destroy that look in her eyes.

A FINE TREMBLING ran through her as Lonen bound her wrists. *Hwil* danced far beyond her grasp as those shameful adolescent desires assaulted her, jumbling with the new ones that centered entirely on Lonen. Naked before her Destrye warrior, vulnerable and at his mercy. He stood close enough that she could turn her hands and run them over his chest, open his shirt and tangle her fingers in the hair beneath. His eyes—a gray so dark they looked almost black in the golden light— flicked up to study her face, the gentle concern a contrast to the raging storm of violent desire beneath. He affected her profoundly on multiple levels, his physical presence amplifying the vivid fantasy images rolling through his mind, of her gasping beneath him, crying out his name, their skin sliding together so slickly she almost felt it.

"If I could," he murmured, voice rasping over her nerves as he walked her backwards, holding only the ends of the silk, "I would be kissing you now. I'd start with light ones, like butterfly wings on your lips, lulling you in until you felt safe enough to open your mouth. Yes, just like that. Your lips wet and plump and pink from meeting mine."

The backs of her thighs hit the edge of the bed, but he kept her from instinctively sitting. Instead he raised her hands above her head, looping her scarf over the rods that held the gauzy bed curtains. Hot blood rioted through her, unruly, exultant, needy. "Lonen…" she whispered.

"You're okay. Just feel. I've got you. By now you'd have opened your mouth to me. My tongue would be inside you, tangling with yours." He left her standing there, arms relaxed, but tethered to the bed. Picking up another scarf from her basket of them, he pressed it to his lips. They looked fuller, more enticing than she'd ever noticed, framed by his glossy black beard. Lifting the scarf to her mouth, he caressed her lower lip with the silk where he'd kissed it, slightly damp from his, tasting of him. "Is this okay?"

So far, yes. Tentatively, she tasted it with the tip of her tongue, finding some of him there. He groaned, eyes hot. "Kitten tongue. I'd pull that into my mouth, maybe nipping at it until you squirmed, begging me for more."

She did squirm, as if his words evoked it, tugging against the silk that only tightened, making her flesh bloom with desire around it. "More. Please give me more."

"Oria," he grated, his hands fisting in the silk. "You might be the death of me."

"Pleasure me, Destrye," she demanded. "Prove your worth to a sorceress of Bára."

He breathed a laugh. "Sweet captive bride, you will writhe for me and, before we're done, you'll scream my name in pleasure."

She wanted to already, convulsing when he drew the silk across her taut nipples. They'd never been so sensitive, her breasts swelling like molten glass, full of breath and fire. Lonen dragged the silk over and around the skin of them, teasing her, while her breath grew ragged.

"These are my lips on you," he told her, picturing it so she would, "licking all this delicious flesh." He stepped back and flicked the ends of the silk against her, drawing incoherent cries in response. "I might use my teeth, too. Do you like that?"

"Yes. Oh, yes." She nearly sobbed the words, unable to take and keep a decent breath. "Whatever you want, warrior."

"Because you belong to me." He loomed large before her, fierce and feral.

Only one answer. "Yes."

"These are my hands on you." Tying the scarf around her rib cage, he knotted above and between her breasts, crossing it up and over her shoulders, then bringing the ends around and beneath, tying them off to the center knot. He took his time, teasing her nipples with the free ends. Picking up her container of mask ribbons, he tied them to the scarves, meticulously making sure not to brush her skin with his, tightening them around her breasts with nearly painful pressure. "I have big hands," he told her as he worked. "Barbarian hands, rough from fighting and manual labor. They scrape your soft white Báran skin and you love it."

"I love it," she agreed, longing for that very thing. "Touch me, Lonen."

"I am. I'm squeezing your breasts. Do you feel that? Taking my fill of you, as is my right."

He tightened the ribbons and she cried out, writhing against the bonds.

"Hold still," he ordered in a harsh voice. "Don't make me bind you further. All your pleading won't save you."

Understanding, she did her best to hold still, transfixed as he made a loop with a thin strip of ribbon, then slipped it over the tight peak of her nipple. His eyes caught hers. "Your teeth chewing your lip—that's me, devouring your mouth, your nipples." Slowly, he tightened the little noose and she gasped at the intensity of it. He smiled, a cruel, ruthless enjoyment of her predicament. "See? Many uses for those ribbons you squander so freely, Princess."

He did the same to her other nipple, all the while describing what he'd be doing to her, until he'd reduced her panting and begging. "Please, Lonen," she chanted.

"You want me between your legs?" he asked, leaning close so his breath caressed her cheek. "Touching you there, making you pump those pretty hips until you can't hold back."

"Yes, yes, yes." She ached there as never before. "Touch me please."

He dropped to his knees, eye level with her sex and she watched him, rapt, abruptly aware that he'd never undressed. "Take off your shirt," she told him.

With a half-smile, he complied. "As you command, Princess." He picked up another scarf, threading it between her ankles and holding the ends in each hand, one in front of her and one behind. Working as slowly as before, he wisped the silk up the inside of her thighs, tantalizing her into edging her feet apart. When he reached the apex of her thighs, he dragged the scarf between her slick nether lips, sliding against her so she whimpered at the intensity of it.

"This is my hand, parting your folds," he whispered. "There, yes?"

She had no words, only moans of encouragement as slipped against her, making her move her hips with it, just as he'd promised. "That's it my hot little princess," he crooned, "take your pleasure from me. My hand stroking you. You feel so good. Here's my mouth on you."

He imagined it, inhaling her scent, and she groaned at the sight of his dark curls between her thighs as the silk worked her. The tension built and she struggled against the mounting pressure. "I want," she panted. "I need."

"Take it then," he rasped. "Let go. Let go of all of it."

"No." She closed her thighs around the silk. "I want all of it. Take me, all the way."

"It's easier to give you pleasure this way and—"

"I don't care. The first time, I want this with you. Make me yours, Destrye."

He rose to his feet, expression intent, ardor swirling about her as if he ran his hands over her flesh indeed. "Shall I plow between your pretty virgin thighs? Take your innocence and make you mine forever more?"

"Yes!" she urged him, all concept of dignity, of reserve in *hwil* vanished. She'd become a wild thing. "Take me. I'm yours to ravish."

He lifted a hand to hover near her cheek, but checked himself from touching her. "So beautiful, my powerful sorceress. So helpless before me." His hand dove into her hair, winding it around his fist and tugging remorselessly so her head tipped back exposing her throat. "Spread your legs for me," he growled.

With a sob, she complied, the opening rocking her apart, with all of her so vulnerable to him. Something touched her thigh, cool and smooth, making her tense. What was it? He tugged her hair and slid it between her nether lips, making her moan, making her forget.

"This is my cock." His voice came harsh and uneven. He pressed it against her aching flesh and pictured crawling between her spread thighs and pushing back her knees, positioning himself at her entrance. "I'm going to take you, my lovely Oria."

"Yes. Lonen. Yes."

He nudged it into her, spreading her slowly, working it back and forth, so she adjusted to the invasion. "This is me, fucking you." In the fantasy he turned her over, holding her hair like the reins of a horse, making her arch her neck even as he pulled her hair in reality, pushing the thing in and out of her. "Keep those pretty thighs spread wide," he cautioned, "or I'll tie them apart. Don't make me hurt you."

Or his hand could brush her skin there, even as carefully as he moved. It felt so good, the filling and stretching, her body quickening, picking up where it had been. She moaned. "I don't care. I want you in me for real. Fuck me for real, Lonen. I don't care if it hurts."

He breathed a wild and ragged laugh. "You would tempt the purest of men to such depravity. Sweet as it will be to sheath myself in you, that day has not yet come. But you're mine just the same. Tell me so."

"I'm yours." She felt it, too, in the syncing of their bodies, the fantasies he fed her and she drank in, pumping back to him with her cries of need and the undulations of her naked body. "With me." The words cracked, so she repeated the demand. "Take yourself in hand and be with me."

With a muttered oath, he released her hair, reaching to undo his leather pants. Avidly she watched him grasp his cock, fisting it as he pumped a like phallus in her. She caught his gaze, the gray catching silver sparks, and poured some of her sgath into him, just a taste, enough to feed his fires. He snarled and pumped harder, a spur of the phallus in her grinding a sensitive spot.

Eyes locked on his, she let go of all reserve. He grunted as he came and—just as he'd promised—she screamed his name when her world split apart.

~ 20 ~

L ONEN FELL TO his knees with the power of the climax, Oria shuddering with the aftershocks of her own orgasm, gleaming like a goddess of fire, her body slick with sweat and sex. His goddess. His queen.

Carefully he slid his dagger hilt from her sweet sex, beyond glad that the wide guard had shielded his hand from her intimate tissues. He'd forgotten himself there at the end, in his excitement, slamming it into her. No blood on her thighs, though, so he'd been right on judging the size. Smaller than his own girth, so easier for her than if he'd penetrated her for the first time. Perhaps by the time they found a way for her to tolerate contact with him, she'd be accustomed enough that he wouldn't hurt her. A good thing, as he'd promised.

Oria smiled at him, stray wisps of hair plastered to her cheeks and temples, her face a perfectly erotic blend of sensuality and satisfaction. Setting the dagger aside, he rose to free her, releasing her from the bed post so she could sit, then untying the bonds around her wrists. She sighed as she plucked the ribbon ties from her nipples and wiggled out of the binding scarves, then flopped back with a gusty breath. Bemused, he watched her as he wiped himself and then the floor where he'd spilled his seed.

Perhaps his seed once parted from his body wouldn't hurt

her, but he hadn't been sure. A man's seed contained a great deal and who knew how it would affect his sensitive Oria. Something they could test, however, in judicious amounts. He might be able to spill his seed on her and work it inside. With something better than his knife hilt. Perhaps he could speak to one of her glass forgers to create a phallus for the purpose. Several of various sizes would be useful, to determine which best pleasured her.

That would be an interesting conversation.

Still, the thought of Oria bearing their heirs lit a fire of hope in him. They would find a way.

Moving carefully, he edged himself onto the bed around her. Lazily, she turned her head, her coppery eyes owlish and sated. "Why aren't you naked?" she asked.

Raising his brows at her, he sat up, shucked off the pants he'd just fastened, along with the boots he'd never gotten around to removing, and rejoined her, obligingly naked as she.

"Lie on your back," she commanded, and he did, bemused, watching her look at him.

"I thought you'd already seen me naked," he reminded her.

"Yes, well." She gave him an impish smile—a delightful one he'd never before seen, that curved her luscious lips and brought dimples to her cheeks—and returned to her scrutiny. "I may have exaggerated. I tried not to look."

"And now?"

She raised her gaze to his again. "I like looking at you. I understand now why you wanted to see me." She gestured at his flaccid cock. "Good thing you didn't have a wound there to tend after all."

He winced at the prospect. "I'll do it, but I won't say I'm not savoring the reprieve."

"I think I could do what you did to yourself," she said, a

hint of shyness in her smile. "Maybe by wrapping cloth around my hands or some such."

His cock stirred at the image. "In Dru we have thick garments for our hands, called gloves, that we wear for warmth. I've thought of that for both of us."

She cocked her head with interest. "I'd like that." She sobered then. "I thought about using grien to touch you, but ...."

"Yeah." He grinned and picked up a lock of her trailing hair, winding it around his finger. "Maybe after you've practiced a bit more. I wouldn't want to be emasculated by my sorceress bride. Think of what the other guys would say."

"Good incentive for you to mind your smart mouth, Destrye," she replied in a tone so arch he wanted to pull her down and drown it with a kiss. She read it in him, her eyes wandering over his face. "I know you don't want me to apologize, but I'm sorry you can't do that, kiss me and touch me for real."

"This is real," he returned. "And it's more than I knew to hope for. You are the burning fire in my heart, Oria."

Her gaze went dewy. "This is more than I imagined to hope for, too."

"Even if I'm not a perfect match for you?" he teased.

She shuddered lightly, a delicious sight on her naked form. "I can't even imagine being like this with anyone but you. Thank you for making this so good for me."

"It's all you, Oria." He fingered the lock of hair. "This would be when we'd cuddle. I'd pull you close against me and hold you in my arms. I'd whisper how sweet and lovely you are, and you would tell me what a huge cock I have."

She burst out laughing and hit him with a pillow. "How about something to eat instead, and then sleep?"

He grinned at her, delighted in everything about her.

"Sounds great. Big day tomorrow."

She stilled in pulling on her chemise. "What are we going to do about the contest?"

"Our best." He tugged her hair. "Between the two of us, that's not inconsiderable."

IN THE MORNING, they descended the stairs together. Oria rested her hand slightly on Lonen's sleeve, where he'd created padding by wrapping his forearms in leather strips. Both for Chuffta to land on and for her to touch, he'd explained, muttering something about similarly sharp talons on each of them that she ignored. Chuffta, riding on her other shoulder, wryly agreed.

She felt too relaxed to rise to Lonen's teasing. Too replete. Though she was sore in places, the slight pain made her feel smug, rather than injured. And not at all fragile. She'd married a man who pleased her well—and with great inventiveness. To her surprise, she discovered she'd begun to believe his assertions that they could triumph over anything. Perhaps they *could* win the contest and the end of the day would see her crowned Queen of Bára.

He'd been right, too, about their increased intimacy. After all they'd done with each other, she felt more at ease with him. Even at his greatest extremity he'd been careful of her, taking her on that wild ride of pleasure beyond anything she'd imagined. He'd relaxed, also, just what he'd declared good sex would do. Even with shadows of caution threading through his thoughts as he contemplated what they faced, his aura radiated satisfied happiness and he shone with confidence.

Also, an idea had occurred to her.

"So," she said quietly, though their voices could hardly carry out of the tower and her sgath revealed no one nearby until the guards at the bottom. The sheer audacity of the idea had her reluctant to speak it too loudly. "I've been thinking. If we're to demonstrate a partnership of sgath and grien, perhaps I can do both. Any grien tricks required of you, I can do, and you can pretend to be generating them."

He gave her a sideways look. "They'd never believe I can work magic. They'd have to know it was you."

She shook her head. "That's it—a woman with grien magic is even more unlikely than a Destrye with it. If they see, they'll believe. There won't be any other explanation."

"Too much risk. We don't dare expose that talent of yours."

"*I agree. Too dangerous,*" Chuffta chimed in, unsolicted.

"This is worth the risk," she argued with both of them. "Otherwise we're certain to lose and I won't be able to wrest control of the Trom from Yar, and both Bára and Dru will be doomed."

Neither of her men liked it, but neither could come up with a better solution.

"Maybe it won't come to that," Lonen said, but the words lacked his usual optimistic confidence.

"I'll save it for a last resort only, I promise."

"I never thought I'd wish for magic," Lonen muttered, then subsided into increasingly brooding thoughts for the remainder of their descent.

Yar and Gallia met them in the courtyard between the palace and temple, along with Priest Vico and a considerable assembly of onlookers from all walks of life. Apparently everyone wanted to witness the show. Juli, who'd been up to help Oria dress and braid her hair, bowed and came to stand behind her as an attendant. No sign of Rhianna, if the former queen had even been told what was going on.

Just as well if not. Even with her aggravation with Yar and disappointment in Oria, it would have to be impossibly difficult to watch your only remaining children duel. For that reason, Oria hadn't sent a message. No matter how this day turned out, their mother would face grief, which she had no ability to withstand.

Another turnabout, for Oria to be strong and her mother so fragile.

Gallia looked as beautifully composed as she had the night before, but her sgath had dimmed, streaked with unhappiness and a sickly pain.

"Are you well, sister?" Oria asked her, after the formal greetings, which Yar rushed through, shimmering grien snaking about him.

Gallia started with surprise. "Very well, thank you. Bára's magic is yet unfamiliar to me. I would not have expected it, but I assimilate Báran sgath differently. It has a … different flavor."

Oria wouldn't have expected that either, but it was interesting. So rarely did the priestesses travel to their sister cities that little information was available regarding such things. "We can postpone the contest if you—"

"Do you seek to delay, sister dear?" Yar ostentatiously took Gallia's bare hand in his. "Perhaps you are afraid and seek to avoid the certain humiliation of defeat. We will accept your forfeit."

"No forfeit," Oria replied, though she didn't like his lack of concern for his new wife. Had Yar always been so self-involved, so callous to the needs of others? Perhaps so. Sometimes what seem to be the flaws of youth are truly the chasms of personality.

"Prepare to be defeated then. Priest Vico—we are ready to begin!" He dropped Gallia's hand as abruptly as he'd seized it, striding over to address the priest.

"Quickly," Oria bent to Gallia. "Whatever should happen today, you will find a champion in our mother, the former queen. She has bad days and good. More of the former than the latter. But visit her regularly, talk with her. You'll learn to anticipate the good days. And if Yar doesn't treat you well, take your appeal to her. She'll help you."

Gallia seemed briefly taken aback before her cloak of *hwil* settled. "I appreciate your concern, sister, but I am content."

Oria doubted it, but she let the woman maintain that façade. Deliberately, she set it aside. She couldn't think of her new sister's plight and maintain the appearance of her own *hwil*.

Lonen brushed a hand over her braids. "She is a sorceress like yourself, not powerless. She'll find a way to handle him."

"Arill make it so," she replied, just so he'd smile. "The onlookers will leave," Priest Vico declared. "Contestants and attendants to remain. Master Chuffta, you may sit to the side."

"The creature helps her," Yar protested. "It's an unfair advantage."

Oria didn't say that she had to be in contact with her Familiar for most of the benefit. If Yar didn't realize that, all the better.

Priest Vico considered. "The derkesthai have a long history of assisting Báran kings and queens. If Princess Oria's Familiar gives her an advantage, then that would go towards her duties as queen as well, and should be ascertained as such. Master

Chuffta may remain."

Oria breathed an internal sigh of relief to at least have Chuffta with her.

"*Always. Even when I'm not physically present, I am with you.*"

"*Unless I'm intimate with Lonen and you're not listening,*" she reminded him.

"*Naturally.*" He managed to keep his mind-voice free of even the least hint of sarcasm. He hadn't commented on her belated wedding night this time, for which she was grateful. Some things weren't for sharing with anyone else. What had passed between her and her Destrye warrior would remain their private secret.

"The contest," announced Priest Vico, "consists of three parts. We begin the first, the demonstration of compatibility."

JUST AS ORIA had predicted. She'd explained to him that the initial testing of compatibility between prospective spouses began with proximity, progressed to casual skin-to-skin contact, and then probably to some form of more intimate contact. She didn't know about the last as she hadn't made it that far with anyone. It perversely pleased him that she hadn't, even though rationally it would be better if she had, and could have known what to prepare them for.

Regardless, this portion would likely be the most difficult for Oria. Her powerful magics weren't in doubt—at least to his eye—only her ability to withstand her husband's touch.

After the onlookers departed at Priest Vico's command, Juli stepped up to cut the ribbons to Oria's mask, while Yar and

Gallia's attendants did likewise. For the first time, Lonen looked on Yar's face, studying his enemy. He had the gawky looks—and unfortunately pimpled skin—of a beardless boy, his eyes strangely dark beneath beetling red brows. Gallia was a lovely woman, with blue eyes and skin more golden than Oria's cream. She took her time blotting her face, her hands unsteady.

"The journey took a toll on her," Oria murmured to him.

"Perhaps last night also," he agreed. It bothered his wife to think of her brother mistreating a woman, though it hardly surprised him, given what he'd seen of Yar's selfish character. Even if he hadn't been deliberately cruel to her, the boy had no compassion in him, no sensitivity to the needs of another person. On top of his likely inexperience with a woman, it made for a bad combination for a virginal bride. Drawing on the hard heart he'd built over years of warfare, he pushed the sympathy aside. "It may sound callous, but if her exhaustion helps our cause…"

"I know." But Oria sounded glum.

"This battle was forced upon us. We didn't choose it, but we'll fight it anyway." If the Destrye had learned nothing else from the Golem Wars, they'd come to understand that truth all too well.

Oria flexed her fingers on his sleeve. "And yet we've both discovered the myriad regrets of the actions we've taken to win those battles. I'd prefer to find a victory that doesn't require another's crushing defeat."

He winced at the reminder that many Bárans had been equally forced into conflict. Now who was selfish? He was saved thinking up an optimistic reply to that by Priest Vico.

"Please embrace your spouse."

Lonen brought Oria into his arms, carefully touching her

over her clothes, postponing the inevitable impact on her. They'd been close when he carried her, but still nothing like this, the lines of their whole bodies folding together. She turned her cheek to lay it against his chest, wrapping slender arms around his waist and nestling against him. Her soft breasts and thighs snuggled into him as if made for him, a slim dagger fitting perfectly into the sheath of his body. Holding her like this reminded him of the first time she'd handed him one of her delicate glass wine vessels—that he might fail to temper his strength and shatter her out of carelessness.

"This is proximity?" he murmured, brushing his lips over the braids crowning her head.

She breathed a laugh. "He skipped a few phases since it's clear we are able to be near each other without suffering."

Indulging himself in the rare luxury, he ran his hands along the elegant line of her spine and dainty curve of her waist. "Is it truly better with me then than it was—being near?"

She raised her face, giving him a small smile. "Better than I ever imagined."

"Remain in physical contact, but take each other's hands, please," Priest Vico instructed.

"Here we go," Lonen muttered, and Oria drew composure about her like a cloak of winter chill.

"Whatever happens, just keep going," she told him. "Don't worry about me. I'll be fine."

He doubted that, and reserved the right to act to protect her according to his own judgment, but he dropped his hands to his sides as she did, lacing his fingers carefully with hers, as if being gentle with her would make any difference. She shuddered, closing her eyes as lines of pain formed around them. She slowed her breathing in a way he recognized now as a method for mastering difficult input. Not unlike a wounded warrior steeling himself against the surgeon's knife.

From what he could tell, she seemed to be doing better than during their wedding ceremony, though that could be entirely false optimism. Especially as bewildering as that experience had been.

Over her head, he met Chuffta's intent gaze, exchanging wordless hope and concern.

Priest Vico might be helping her as Lonen hoped, because he wasted little time making Oria endure the contact. "And now a kiss, maintained until I ask you to stop."

Number three. At least the trial would stop at a kiss. Not what Lonen had hoped for their first kiss, but so it went in their star-crossed marriage. Oria raised her face, lines of strain between her brows and bracketing her lovely mouth. "Stop fretting," she taunted. "Chicken."

Arill, how he loved this woman. Delay only made it worse, so he brushed her lips with his, unable to savor the sweetness of her with the incoherent sound of pain she made. Doing his best to shield her, he held back his emotions as he would on the battlefield. Her heart pounded in frantic beats, shuddering into him, and he kissed her softly, soothingly, if only to make that aspect as bearable as possible.

A scuffle and cry in the background. "Beast!" Gallia cried. Adhering to the rules, Lonen kept the kiss, ignoring whatever had happened. If Yar and Gallia forfeited, so much the better.

"You may desist," Priest Vico called in a placid tone as if nothing had happened.

Oria broke away from him, gasping for breath, clutching her hands to her stomach as if she might be ill. He checked his impulse to reach for her, to comfort her, clenching his hands into fists instead. So wrong that what should be good between them was the worst thing for her.

"Both marriages pass the compatibility test," the priest declared.

"Are you insane?" Yar thrust a finger in Oria's direction. "Look at her. She's staggering from the impact of that barbarian's foul touch."

"Look to your own bride, Prince Yar," the priest replied. "Impacts occur on many levels. However, I concede that Prince Yar and Priestess Gallia demonstrate greater compatibility, so far as magic is concerned."

A fine point, as Gallia, while not obviously physically stressed as Oria, looked miserably unhappy, a trickle of blood at the corner of her mouth. She took the cloth her attendant offered, wiping it away and seemed grateful to don her mask again.

Oria did too, quietly talking with Juli as she did so. With a pang that he refused to accept as foreboding, he watched her face disappear behind the featureless metal again.

LONEN WORRIED FOR her palpably, his concern tugging at her, but she couldn't reassure him. At this point, she could only grit through. He'd been as gentle as possible with her, but the contact, particularly mouth to mouth, had burned like acid, hollowing her out as surely as if he'd taken his axe to her. If she thought about it too much, she'd become depressed at the unlikelihood of them ever being able to touch with pleasure. A small consideration, perhaps, given the far more daunting obstacles they faced, but one that had become strangely important to her.

"Yesterday you were certain you could not lie with him at all and you have. Give it time. You're doing brilliantly well."

Grateful for her Familiar, she sent him a loving thought and straightened, moving to Lonen and putting her hand on his padded forearm.

"I'm so sorry," he murmured.

"No apologies," she reminded him.

He growled under his breath but subsided when Vico spoke.

"For the second part, the priestesses will demonstrate their sgath. Please, gather your sgath and offer it to Grienon through me. Would either of you prefer to go first?"

"I'll go first," Oria said, ignoring Lonen's muttered protest. Yes, she was giving Gallia time to sort herself, but she couldn't do less. Even though Oria had focused on Lonen's kiss, trying to ignore the pain of contact in favor of the surprisingly lovely tickle of his beard on her face, the shocking tender heat of his mouth—her sgath had relentlessly revealed how harshly Yar had kissed his new bride. Lonen was likely right that she should treat Gallia as the enemy, but her heart ached for her sister.

And she was so very weary of having enemies.

Also, this part at least came easily to her now. Accumulating sgath had never been the problem for her—quite the opposite. Until the night before when she'd completely depleted herself. For the most part, once she'd learned how to see and hold it comfortably, all those lessons on connecting it to a priest fell into place. Breathing in the clean, clear, and familiar magic of Bára, Sgatha's gift, she let it well up into a serene pool, and presented it to Priest Vico. In the same way, the priestesses of the city had offered their collective sgath to the battle mages.

Priest Vico sipped from it, then bowed in thanks, and spoke the ritual words. "A powerful gift, indeed. I thank you, priestess, for sharing with this humble priest."

Yar seethed, his grien energy sparking and swirling in her mind's eye. Her own grien wanted to rise to battle it, but she restrained it. Soon enough. He nudged Gallia forward. "Show him. Gallia is the most powerful junior priestess of Lousá. She will make a great queen."

Perhaps so, but at that moment her sgath hung in a ragged mist. Oria choked back her sympathy for the woman as she tried to reach for Bára's unfamiliar magic. It seemed to slip away from her the moment she reached for it, like a skittish kitten uncertain of a stranger and unwilling to be petted just yet. What she did manage to gather, the dark cavities of the journey's strain devoured as quickly as she built it up. Yar was an idiot to have pushed her so fast. She finally pulled together enough to offer Priest Vico, who thanked her as he had Oria.

"While Priestess Gallia's sgath is present, Priestess Oria's strength of sgath is far greater. This part goes to her and King Lonen."

Yar took Gallia's arm, shaking her slightly as he spoke in an undertone to her. His grien lashed about her, but she appeared unmoved. Enviable *hwil*.

"For the third part, the priests will demonstrate their grien," Vico declared. "Please, focus your grien and release it according to your affinity, but in a way that all might observe, to please Sgatha. Would either of you—"

"I might as well go." Yar swaggered as he stepped forward. "As we know how this will end."

He raised his hands, his powerful grien streaming out. With careless effort, he drew from the stone of the chasm and the rock spires behind the temple's towers, sculpting a column, then refining it.

Into a statue of himself as king.

Safe in the anonymity of her mask, Oria rolled her eyes at his hubris. She couldn't stand by and allow him to take the throne. That had long been her resolve, but the day's events—and seeing how he abused the woman he should cherish—only reinforced her certainty. Even if they lost this trial, she would find another way to defeat her brother.

Not only for the Destrye, for Lonen, and for Bára, but for the good of the world.

Yar twirled and bowed, making an insult of the demonstration. Priest Vico acknowledged his grien with the ritual words neutrally enough, but her brother's accomplishment spoke volumes. Even among her family, even compared to their father the king, Yar's gift had stood out in both its strength and his skill with it. If only he had something of Lonen's character, he might be worthy of such power.

As it was, the prospect of him with the rule of Bára and full access to the temple secrets soured her gut. She simply could not fail. The stakes were far too high.

"King Lonen?" the priest invited.

"Why bother?" Yar sounded bored. "He's a mind-dead barbarian grunt. He has nothing to demonstrate. I've won. Two out of three."

"Not true," Oria answered the challenge. She'd learned the value of magic well-faked. "The Destrye have magic of their own and King Lonen will demonstrate it."

"Oria, no," Lonen urged in a low voice, his emotions anything but quiet. "It's not worth the risk. We'll find another way."

"I'm doing it," she replied in an even tone. "Play along or you will have blown it for us before we've begun."

~ 21 ~

H E WANTED TO fight her on it, but recognized the utter futility. Perhaps he'd been wrong in thinking—bragging even—that he possessed more stubbornness. Obstinacy or will, Oria had cultivated an ability to forge ahead regardless of the consequences to herself. And now her survival depended on him making a convincing show of working Destrye magic.

His father and brothers must be howling with laughter as they watched from the Hall of Warriors. At least he provided entertainment for them. A Destrye pretending to be a sorcerer. If the poets didn't write ballads proclaiming him a fool for taking a Báran sorceress to wife, they surely would for this fiasco.

With no idea what he'd do—he should have realized Oria would insist on this reckless strategy and planned ahead—he unstrapped his battle axe and began swinging it in the basic training cycle, chanting a nonsense rhyme of Destrye children, which would hopefully sound like a magical incantation. More fodder for that future ballad.

"Heya naya, frahm frahm frinny. Naya heya, frinnah say say."

He repeated it, moving the axe from hand to hand, adding in foot stomping as if he danced to Destrye drums. The sweep of Oria's magic filtered through him, tingling as it had when she'd teased his cock with it, but passing through and to the laughable edifice Yar had created. It creaked and shivered, then burst with vines, twining and trailing with rapid growth. Huge indigo flower buds swelled, then burst in blossom. The vines turned woody, encasing and obscuring the sculpture's lines until it was unrecognizable.

Drawing the line there, lest Oria take it in her head to do more and even further risk exposing herself, Lonen set down his axe and wiped his brow.

Priest Vico regarded him, surprise in the lines of his shoulders. "Bára will benefit from nature magic such as yours, King Lonen. I've never seen its like, not even in the temple annals. The Destrye appear to have secrets of their own. Both men have demonstrated the application of magic. While Prince Yar's grien is more powerful and he demonstrated more refined skill with it, King Lonen's is unique and much needed in this time of privation. This part goes to—"

"Wait." Yar held up a hand, regal command in his voice, all trace of the arrogant boy gone. "Oria, forfeit. Do it now or I will speak the truth of this."

Dread coiled in Lonen's stomach. Yar did know, as Oria had feared, and he would use that knowledge to win. So be it. At least her brother had shown some filial compassion and given her an out.

"I have no intention of forfeiting," Oria replied, equally cool, devastating Lonen with the words. "The contest will be won fairly or not at all."

"Don't make me do this." Yar actually sounded human again. A boy not ready for the pressures he'd shouldered. "I don't want your death. Forfeit."

Priest Vico looked between them. "Her death?"

"Last chance, Oria. Forfeit or die."

Lonen turned to Oria, mentally urging her to do it with everything in him, speaking as loudly as he dared. "We'll find another way, Oria. It's not worth it. Take the out. Forfeit."

"Is that what you would do?" she replied under her breath. "You who stormed the walls of Bára by yourself? I think not. I refuse to be a coward."

No time to argue he'd not been entirely alone. "It's not cowardice to retreat in the face of doom, to leave the field of battle to fight another day. You can't fight him if you're dead."

"He can't prove anything," she insisted. "It's a bluff."

He couldn't take the chance. Not with her life and not with the future of his people hanging in the balance. "I'm sorry to do this, but I can't let you risk this."

"Don't you dare!" she snarled, her magic whipping at him.

He ignored her, raising his voice. "We forfeit."

But Priest Vico shook his head. "The contest is between Prince Yar and Princess Oria. Only they can forfeit. Do you wish to forfeit, Princess?"

"No. Pronounce your determination."

"Very well, the contest goes to Queen Oria and her consort King Lonen. May you reign in—"

"Remember that you forced my hand, Oria," Yar cut through. "The grien is hers." The words thudded flat into sudden, shocked silence.

Priest Vico visibly floundered. "The... the what you say?"

"The grien. It's hers. She's an abomination and should be executed as such. High Priestess Febe knew it and Oria killed her to keep the secret. Oria used it against me before today and like a sentimental fool I protected her and did not report it to the temple. I take full responsibility for my lapse."

"Ridiculous," Oria sneered. "No woman can use grien. It's not an abomination; it's an impossibility."

"Examine her," Yar told the priest. "If you look closely, you can see it in her. I can see it now. Revolting and against nature, but there."

Oria stiffened as Priest Vico approached her. "Forgive me, Princess, but temple law compels me to be certain that such an anomaly has not occurred."

HER PREVIOUS CONFIDENCE bled away, leaving fear behind. Much of it came from Lonen and she abruptly regretted her foolhardy bravado. If she failed this examination, she'd fail again to keep her word to aid the Destrye—and this time through her own actions.

All because she simply could not force herself to swallow her pride and forfeit to Yar.

"Can you help me?" she sent to Chuffta, fully aware she grasped at sand already blown away.

"I don't know how I can." His mind-voice sounded afraid also. *"Be still and serene as possible. Focus on sgath, bring that aspect up as strong as you can."*

She did her best, silencing the frantic whispers of her over-sensitized nerves that hadn't at all settled from the stress of the compatibility test. Beating frantically against her ribs, her heart thrummed like a trapped jewelbird. Though Lonen tried to drown his emotions behind the image of that serene lake, his worry threaded toward her. She couldn't think about him.

Except that if she died, he'd at least be free to marry Natly and have a normal wife he could bed. No, that thought didn't help because she wasn't that generous. Lonen was her husband

and she wanted to live, to keep him and see that lake for herself, to learn to swim in it.

Besides, without her Yar's Trom would kill them all. She had to win this. She was on the side of the good and right. Surely that meant something.

It wasn't fair that they'd lose because she couldn't conceal a simple bit of magic. The silence stretched on. Then Priest Vico's astonishment and deep regret flooded her senses.

"Former priestess Oria," he said at last, his voice hushed and hoarse. "You are disqualified from this contest. I must ask that you surrender your mask."

Gallia made a sound and Oria appreciated her new sister's sympathy. Or perhaps it was revulsion. In the end, it likely didn't matter. She tried to think of a solution, a defense, some way to extract herself from this, but came up with nothing nothing nothing.

With fingers as numb as her brain, she fumbled at the ribbons, grateful when Lonen stepped up to undo the knots for her, his bedrock strength as steady as ever. Juli took the mask, her sgath curling in comforting tendrils. Vico accepted it from her and turned his back decisively on Oria.

"King Yar and Queen Gallia, may you reign in peace," he declared.

Yar's grien rocketed in bolts of triumph, lashing out to shiver over the stone statue of himself, fragments of stone sifting down and taking her leaves and blossoms with them. The cleaned stone stood starkly clean when he'd finished, its sterility an apt foreshadowing of their futures.

"I only regret that my first action as king will be my sister's execution." He almost managed to sound sorry about it. "It's your fault, Oria, for driving me to this."

"An ill omen to begin a new era," Priest Vico noted, without emotion, his *hwil* perfect.

"Is it?" Yar rounded on the priest, his voice and grien turned snarling. "You dare criticize me? I say it's a good omen. We begin my reign on a fresh page, with Bára cleansed anew of the abominations perpetuated on our fair city. I will make Bára great again!"

"Be careful, kingling," Lonen ground out from just behind her shoulder. "You are still my subject, Bára belongs to Dru as Princess Oria belongs to me. I am the final law here and you will not gainsay me or I will bring devastation down upon you and destroy your city, great or not."

Oria nearly protested, but Lonen put a firm hand on her shoulder, and she subsided. He'd given her room to do what she thought best and she'd failed him. She owed him whatever steps he wished to take now.

"Your words are but sand on the breeze," Yar returned. "You have no idea of the power I wield, Destrye. Run home to your pitiful forests and ruined crops. Plant more. I'll simply burn them again. I care not for your fate."

With a snarl of rage, Lonen stepped around her, axe at the ready. Yar met it with a blast of grien that made the Destrye stagger. Snapping out of her fog of stunned grief, Oria put herself between them, creating a wall of grien of her own to protect them.

Yar clenched his fists and howled in frustration. "Gallia! Feed me sgath. We cannot allow this renegade abomination to escape." He reached for her, but Gallia stepped back, releasing the sgath she'd replenished in the interim, sending it to Oria through a path so subtle only another woman would be able to detect it.

"I'm sorry, my husband," she answered in a thready voice, as if terribly weakened. "I hate to fail you, but I have nothing to offer. I cannot help."

Yar rounded on her, fist upraised, but she knelt in apology. Her mind-voice whispered into Oria's, astonishing her. *"Run, sister. Take your life and go. Survive outside the walls. Bára and Lousá await your return."*

"That's our cue." Even as Lonen spoke the words, he swept Oria up, tossing her over his shoulder and taking off at a run, axe still in hand. Had she been able to appreciate the irony of it, she would have laughed at the image they must make. Straight out of the illustrations. Except for Chuffta faithfully winging behind them, fierce and ready to burn anyone who tried to stop them.

"But where will we go?" she gasped, the words stuttering out with his pounding strides. Even in his haste, he carefully didn't touch her skin. *Survive outside the walls. Bára and Lousá await your return.* Was it possible? Did she have any choice?

"Anywhere but this place," he snapped back. "Just hold the cursed wall so he can't follow. You do your part, I'll do mine."

It was, she supposed, what they'd agreed to all along.

Thank you for reading! I hope you loved the continuing adventures of Oria and Lonen—and Chuffta! The next book in the Sorcerous Moons series is *The Tides of Bára*. Will Lonen and Oria survive the lethal deserts?

"Loving how the passion and love is building between Lonen and Oria! The sex is very hot and interesting… They have to fight some very dangerous battles and make hard choices. Trust is building. Danger lurking everywhere. I also adore Chaffta! He made me laugh and want a pet dragon of my own!"

~Storyweaver

I appreciate your help in spreading the word about my books, including telling a friend or leaving a review. Reviews help readers find books! I'd love it if you'd leave a review on your favorite site.

SIGN UP FOR JEFFE KENNEDY'S NEWSLETTER for fun giveaways from Jeffe and other authors. landing.mailerlite.com/webforms/landing/r2y4b9

Turn the page for a short excerpt from *The Tides of Bára*.

~ 1 ~

ORIA HELD THE barrier against her raging brother.

At least, she did the best she could with her magic draining by the moment, its potency attenuating with distance and diminishing with the lack of opportunity to replenish her sgath—or to even take a full breath. Of course, her upside-down position, bouncing over Lonen's shoulder as he ran headlong through the palace, did nothing to make any of it easier.

"We may be in luck," Chuffta, her Familiar, reported. *"Yar's magic is running low also. He's sent for more priestesses to feed him sgath, as Gallia can't."* He paused to mentally cough at that. Oria's Familiar had also telepathically received Gallia's urgent message for them to run. As Yar's wife—particularly a newlywed in a temple-blessed marriage—only Gallia should be feeding Yar sgath to fight the magical barrier Oria had erected to save herself from execution, and Lonen from retribution. But Gallia had only recently arrived in Bára and, unused to the city's native magic, so different from her home at Lousá, she had not reached her full power.

But Gallia was stronger than she'd claimed. As a sister in magic, Oria could judge quite precisely how much Gallia had been capable of channeling. Oria's new sister had exaggerated her weakness—in a move shockingly disloyal to her new husband and against all expectation—to allow Oria to escape. If all went well, Yar would never discover the deception. Between his unstable temper and Gallia's status in Bára, that could turn out badly for her sister sorceress. Hopefully, she'd take Oria's advice and appeal to her and Yar's mother, the former Queen Rhianna, for assistance.

"I can't imagine Priest Vico will allow other priestesses to feed sgath to Yar. It's against temple law if his ideal wife is alive and well," she replied to Chuffta.

"Yes, but it depends on what Vico considers to be 'well.'"

She framed a reply—speaking mentally took concentration—then grunted in pain as Lonen ducked around a corner, the sudden shift in direction making his shoulder dig into her belly. It looked so much more romantic in the illustrations. In reality, being carried off over a barbarian's shoulder left much to be desired.

"Sorry," Lonen shot the word out between panting breaths. "Unavoidable."

She didn't reply. Couldn't. It would be handy if she and Lonen could speak mind-to-mind the way she could with Chuffta—and unexpectedly with Gallia—particularly under circumstances like this. He might not like it, though. At the moment, all of his considerable personal energy was focused away from her, no doubt on fighting them free of Bára. At least that saved her having to screen out his emotions along with everyone else's.

"You are correct," Chuffta reported from his vantage, flying well above Yar's group. Her Familiar seemed to be enjoying his spy activities. *"They are arguing about it. Yar is most put out. He's losing focus and less able to fight your barrier. Vico is gently suggesting he check his* hwil, *which has not gone over well."* No, Yar would not do well with the suggestion that he might be

showing any loss of the crucial equanimity that allowed the priests and priestesses of Bára to handle their dangerously powerful magic. Loss of *hwil* could be grounds for the temple taking back the mask that was their badge of office. With no mask, Yar could not be king. Could she somehow use that to her advantage—push Yar into losing *hwil* entirely?

"*No, Oria.*" Chuffta's mind-voice was both sorrowful and deadly earnest. "*Without your mask, you cannot be queen either. And now that they know you can use grien, your life would be forfeit, regardless. It's not worth the risk.*"

It might be, though. If only to save Bára and Dru both from the devastation that would be Yar's rule.

"*I won't let you sacrifice yourself. Neither will Lonen,*" Chuffta added.

"*I'm already regretting that I encouraged you two to become friends,*" she grumbled.

TITLES BY JEFFE KENNEDY

FANTASY ROMANCES

BONDS OF MAGIC
Dark Wizard
Bright Familiar
Grey Magic
Familiar Winter Magic (In Fire of the Frost)

HEIRS OF MAGIC
The Long Night of the Crystalline Moon
(also available in *Under a Winter Sky*)
The Golden Gryphon and the Bear Prince
The Sorceress Queen and the Pirate Rogue
The Dragon's Daughter and the Winter Mage
The Storm Princess and the Raven King (May 2022)

THE FORGOTTEN EMPIRES
The Orchid Throne
The Fiery Crown
The Promised Queen

THE TWELVE KINGDOMS
Negotiation

The Mark of the Tala
The Tears of the Rose
The Talon of the Hawk
Heart's Blood
The Crown of the Queen

THE UNCHARTED REALMS
The Pages of the Mind
The Edge of the Blade
The Snows of Windroven
The Shift of the Tide
The Arrows of the Heart
The Dragons of Summer
The Fate of the Tala
The Lost Princess Returns

THE CHRONICLES OF DASNARIA
Prisoner of the Crown
Exile of the Seas
Warrior of the World

SORCEROUS MOONS
Lonen's War
Oria's Gambit
The Tides of Bára
The Forests of Dru
Oria's Enchantment
Lonen's Reign

A COVENANT OF THORNS
Rogue's Pawn
Rogue's Possession
Rogue's Paradise

CONTEMPORARY ROMANCES

Shooting Star

MISSED CONNECTIONS
Last Dance
With a Prince
Since Last Christmas

CONTEMPORARY EROTIC ROMANCES

Exact Warm Unholy
The Devil's Doorbell

FACETS OF PASSION
Sapphire
Platinum
Ruby
Five Golden Rings

FALLING UNDER
Going Under
Under His Touch
Under Contract

EROTIC PARANORMAL

MASTER OF THE OPERA E-SERIAL
Master of the Opera, Act 1: Passionate Overture
Master of the Opera, Act 2: Ghost Aria
Master of the Opera, Act 3: Phantom Serenade
Master of the Opera, Act 4: Dark Interlude
Master of the Opera, Act 5: A Haunting Duet
Master of the Opera, Act 6: Crescendo
Master of the Opera

BLOOD CURRENCY

Blood Currency

<u>BDSM FAIRYTALE ROMANCE</u>

Petals and Thorns

Thank you for reading!

ABOUT JEFFE KENNEDY

Jeffe Kennedy is a multi-award-winning and best-selling author of romantic fantasy. She is the current President of the Science Fiction and Fantasy Writers of America (SFWA) and is a member of Romance Writers of America (RWA), and Novelists, Inc. (NINC). She is best known for her RITA® Award-winning novel, *The Pages of the Mind*, the recent trilogy, *The Forgotten Empires*, and the wildly popular, *Dark Wizard*. Jeffe lives in Santa Fe, New Mexico.

Jeffe can be found online at her website: JeffeKennedy.com, on her podcast First Cup of Coffee, every Sunday at the popular SFF Seven blog, on Facebook, on Goodreads, on BookBub, and pretty much constantly on Twitter @jeffekennedy. She is represented by Sarah Younger of Nancy Yost Literary Agency.

jeffekennedy.com
facebook.com/Author.Jeffe.Kennedy
twitter.com/jeffekennedy
goodreads.com/author/show/1014374.Jeffe_Kennedy
bookbub.com/profile/jeffe-kennedy

Sign up for her newsletter here.
jeffekennedy.com/sign-up-for-my-newsletter